N

THE GUNS OF TRASK

Desperately seeking a place to rest, a weary gunfighter rides over a bleak mountain and discovers a fertile valley. For twenty years this man had owned a unique pair of hand-tooled colts, and he had become known as the legendary Trask. Now he begins to fear the weapons which had never failed him. Riding deeper into the beautiful valley he is about to find out that, even here, there will be no peace for him — evil will ruthlessly seek out and challenge the guns of Trask.

Books by Michael D. George
in the Linford Western Library:

THE VALLEY OF DEATH
THE WAY STATION
DEATH ON THE DIXIE
KID PALOMINO
RIDERS OF THE BAR 10
IRON EYES

MICHAEL D. GEORGE

THE GUNS OF TRASK

Complete and Unabridged

LINFORD
Leicester

First published in Great Britain in 2000 by
Robert Hale Limited
London

NE 2/8/02

First Linford Edition
published 2002
by arrangement with
Robert Hale Limited
London

The moral right of the author has been asserted

British Library CIP Data

George, Michael D.
  The guns of Trask.—Large print ed.—
Linford western library
  1. Western stories
  2. Large type books
  I. Title
  823.9′14 [F]

ISBN 0–7089–9765–1

UKV   12/6/02

Published by
F. A. Thorpe (Publishing)
Anstey, Leicestershire

Set by Words & Graphics Ltd.
Anstey, Leicestershire
Printed and bound in Great Britain by
T. J. International Ltd., Padstow, Cornwall

This book is printed on acid-free paper

Dedicated to my pal Red

Prologue

There are those who blame their tools when disaster strikes. In the same way, skilled craftsmen can create wondrous objects with only their own ability to assist them. Legends are often created around people or objects and over the years confusion blurs the facts.

In the legends of ancient times, was King Arthur a truly great leader who had a sword called Excalibur, or could it have been the sword itself which made an ordinary man become great?

Some achieve greatness and take the full credit themselves whilst others see a mystical intervention in their success.

When one young man buys a pair of guns that sit in hand-tooled holsters upon a thick leather belt with the simple name of TRASK branded into it, he finds that nobody can match his skill with these weapons.

1

As the years roll on, the man matures and becomes known by the name of Trask. Without ever trying, he is famed throughout the West for his unmatched ability with the two guns and yet he is troubled.

No matter how far he rides he can find no peace and begins to wonder about the gun-belt which he innocently purchased two decades earlier.

Who was Trask?

How many other men had become known as Trask before him?

The most serious question of all: was it he who was truly skilled with those two beautiful pistols, or was he merely the man who held them in his hands?

Perhaps it was the guns themselves that never missed their targets and he was simply their present guardian. Just an ordinary man wearing an extraordinary gunbelt. Perhaps he was merely the tool used by the guns.

After more than twenty years seeking answers, the now mature man wondered whether his life had been blessed or cursed the day he first set eyes upon the guns in their leather holsters. He was still alive, but had little else to show for all those years of continually moving.

Whatever the truth, the man known as Trask felt certain that soon he would find the answer.

Was it he who was an expert with pistols or was it actually the guns of Trask?

1

It was a wondrous valley the rider gazed
down upon as his tall chestnut stallion
paused on the high mountain trail.
Staring down, the dust-caked rider
knew that this might be a place where
he could finally find peace. It had been
a long ride that seemed to have taken
most of his grown days to complete yet
it had been worth it, for the most part.
This might be the end of the trail and a
chance to hang up his guns forever.
This valley sure looked like it had room
for him. Stepping off the tired horse he
stretched his weary bones until he felt
everything clicking back into place once
more. There was a small town nestling
in the heart of the fertile green valley.
Smoke rose from the red-brick stacks
that edged the sides of the buildings
giving the place a lived-in look.

The sky had a blue that the tired eyes

of the man had not seen for many a long year. Perhaps, it was bluer than any sky he had ever witnessed before. Filling his Stetson with water from his canteen he rested it between the faithful mount's forelegs. The chestnut drank noisily as he rested against the mountain wall rubbing the dried grime from his features. The man looked at his lathered-up horse knowing that the creature would have ridden until his heart burst if he had commanded it. There were few horses better and few as brave. His eyes drifted to the saddle and the scabbard holding his Winchester. Then he looked at his gun-belt hanging on the saddle horn with its pair of hand-tooled holsters holding the two pistols that had served him well over the years. The Eagle-Butt Peacemaker .45s with their beautiful mother-of-pearl grips sporting the design of an eagle fighting a rattler, and silver-plated bodies with seven-inch barrels.

The guns looked harmless enough as they lay covered in trail dust in their holsters. That was perhaps the problem which had kept him riding from one place to another seeking peace. He had used those guns with such skill that they had become who he truly was. It had been twenty or more years since he first strapped on that rig and tied the hanging leather laces around his thighs. He had never needed to practise with the twin pistols. From that first day, he had been fast and accurate with them. As if he had been incomplete until he had found them.

The man finished off what was left in his canteen and screwed the stopper back on before walking to the saddle horn and hanging the empty canteen over it. His eyes stared at the gunbelt as if looking at something he had loved and hated with equal emotion.

Then he raised his hands and rubbed at the baked dust until it started to fall away from the leather and dropped onto the soil at his feet. A final blow with his cracked lips revealed the name that was branded into the leather belt below the line of cartridges. His eyes narrowed as he stared at the name which had now become his own, TRASK. It had been many a long year since he had first seen the gleaming guns sitting proudly in the hand-crafted holsters and the broad belt. Many years since he had first set his once youthful stare upon that branded name. So many years that he had almost forgotten what he had once been called. When he had purchased these guns they had taken over his life. He had become Trask. These were his guns. These were the guns of Trask.

The man leaned on the saddle, thoughtfully considering the years that had passed before this moment. He wondered whether his life might have been better had he not stepped into the hardware store back in Cheyenne two decades earlier and bought these two beautiful pistols. It was a question that had haunted Trask for half of those years. He had become famous, or maybe just infamous over the years and the wild territories that he had wandered, but it had not served him well. Now he wondered if his days of riding were through. His face now lined by the passing years seemed to regret all that had gone before this day. The guns of Trask had never missed their chosen targets, never let him down and yet he feared them.

Who had been Trask before he had strapped on the fine leather belt? How many Trasks had there been? A cold shiver made the tired man shake for an instant as if someone had walked over his grave. How long had he before the guns wanted a newer, younger, fresher owner?

There were only so many places he could go and it seemed he had visited them all. Trask had never been a man for returning to old trails. He had never gone back to anywhere that he had previously visited. Young faces of his youth might now display their inevitable ageing to eyes unwilling to accept the passing of so many hard years.

9

Trask had continued riding to newer pastures seeking something that might never be found. Memories were his only companions. To go back would be to allow the truth to invade his thoughts.

Staring down into the green luscious valley as the morning sunlight spread across it, he began to wonder if he might just be able to quit his constant quest. Trask retrieved his Stetson and placed it onto his greying hair before taking up the reins once more and mounting the chestnut. The air seemed to taste of honey in his dry mouth. Had he finally found the place that he had ridden so long searching for? The sweet valley seemed so peaceful to tired weary eyes and yet he had been disappointed, before. Tapping his spurs into the horse Trask aimed the tired animal at the trail ahead of him. Slowly Trask rode down the slope into this beautiful place.

He had two silver dollars to his name tucked safely into his jacket pocket. Enough for a meal and a couple of drinks. Then he would have to find work. The small town drew him closer with every beat of his stallion's heart as he descended gradually from the high mountain pass.

The ride soon brought him into the valley which was filled with broad-leafed trees that obscured his view of what lay ahead on the twisting trail. It was far warmer on the valley floor compared to the high mountain pass he had taken so long to navigate.

Trask allowed the chestnut to find its own speed along the strange peaceful avenue. The trail seemed seldom used as Trask rode on. For over an hour the horse continued along the trail that wove its way peacefully through the tall trees. Occasionally there were fields and meadows filled with tall grass and wildflowers of a thousand colours. For over an hour he had ridden the chestnut stallion without seeing another living person and that suited him fine. He knew it was a long journey to the distant town he had seen so clearly from his vantage point on the top of the mountain pass. Trask was in no hurry to find the town because he was finding the valley a refreshing change to the hard cruel ride that had caused him to take to the high lonesome mountain peak.

Trask rode calmly allowing the horse to dictate its own pace when he heard the welcome sound of a fresh stream just off the side of the dirt road. Pulling up, Trask dismounted and led the horse down into the soft mud and allowed the creature to drink its fill of the ice-cold water that came from the mountain above the valley. He sat for a while next to the clear cool stream before filling his canteen. The air was alive with the sounds of contented creatures as Trask rested. Thoughts of what lay behind him over the tall mountain filled him with concern. Sitting in the shadows he could just see the peak of the mountain through the swaying branches above his head.

Trask remounted and rode the

refreshed horse back up onto the trail and resumed his ride. The chestnut had a new spring in its step after standing in the cold mountain stream. For another ten minutes the ride was uneventful, then to his surprise he heard a blood-chilling sound ahead of him. Pulling his reins hard, Trask stopped the powerful horse and stood in his stirrups rubbing the beast's sweating neck with his right hand as he gripped the reins tightly with his left.

Trask listened and could make something out. The noise drifted back on the gentle fresh breeze and instantly became recognizable to Trask's ears: it was the sound of a woman calling for help.

Sitting back down he slapped the reins hard. The stallion thundered forward with Trask gritting his teeth as they took the first bend at incredible speed. Then he saw the buckboard racing across a meadow of tall green grass with its hapless passenger sitting helplessly on the driver's seat next to a man who was slumped across her lap.

As Trask drove his horse on he could see the long reins of the buckboard were trailing underneath the wheels. Racing on, Trask spurred his mount and chased the runaway vehicle across the meadow as its matched pair of sorrels charged towards a distant line of trees. Trask could see that there was no way through the massive trees as he turned the chestnut hard to try and intercept the buckboard.

The stallion thundered across the grassland with its rider sticking to the saddle as if glued on. Jumping a three-foot wide ditch, the horse continued gaining on the reckless buckboard with every stride of its long agile legs. Trask pulled at his reins and steered the chestnut directly at the lead horse.

Finding a turn of speed from the very depths of its soul, the massive stallion drew level with the accelerating four-wheeler allowing Trask to lean towards the sorrels' bridles. His first grab at the leather rigging failed and Trask had to balance himself again as he could see the wall of trees getting dangerously close. He leaned from his saddle again and grabbed at the leather blinkers and, using every sinew in his right arm, pulled the horse's head back until it started to slow. Within seconds, the buckboard rolled to a halt enabling the rider to release his grip.

Dismounting Trask moved to the buckboard and quickly climbed up the driver's side of the large wooden vehicle pulling on the massive brake pole.

Checking the driver, Trask found his hands covered in blood as he pulled the lifeless body off the female's lap. He stared at his hands before heaving the driver around. Only then did Trask see the knife embedded between the shoulder blades. His shocked expression soon found the shaking stare of the female whose screams had first alerted him to the situation.

Trask looked at the woman hard and long with eyes that showed he had not seen many finely dressed ladies lately. 'Ma'am,' he said in a low drawl that told her he was not from these parts.

'Thank you, sir. Thank you.' Her voice trembled with a mixture of shock and fear.

'You OK?' Trask tried to reassure her that her ordeal was over even if the questions were not.

She nodded and cast her eyes down upon her once pristine dress that now was soaked in the blood of the driver. There was suddenly an outburst of emotion that sent her fleeing down from the buckboard through the long grass. Trask jumped down and ran after her. He somehow managed to catch and turn her to face him. To his surprise she fell into his dust-covered body and wept for several minutes until she was empty of tears and his shirt front was soaking wet. Only then did she move away and dry her eyes with a lace handkerchief.

'How did that man get a knife in his back, ma'am?' Trask asked, taking off his Stetson and rubbing his temple with his sleeve.

There was a look of total disbelief etched on her beautiful face. 'My father and I were out riding, as is our habit on fine mornings. Someone must have been hiding in the bushes. I heard him groan and then he slumped over losing the reins. The team went wild and bolted.'

Trask walked around her before staring at the incredible scenery. It seemed impossible that anyone in such a place could be so murderous, yet the evidence was lying dead on the driving seat of the tall vehicle. 'My name's Trask. I'm willing to drive you into town if you like.'

She dried her face before staring at him. 'I'm Juliette Hart and that was my father, Thomas.'

Trask moved to the buckboard and climbed it. Carefully he lifted the old man off the seat and lay him down on the flat bed. Using his sleeve he cleaned the seat as best he could before

17

covering the old man with his jacket. Staring down at the woman standing in the tall grass he felt angry. Angry that some killer could hurt her.

It had been a long time since Trask had felt any emotion for anyone else apart from himself. Being selfish had become second nature to him as he had drifted aimlessly from one town to the next across the endless west. Taking care of number one had been his only concern for so many years that he could not recall when that had started. Once he had never refused anyone any help they required. He had never asked for pay, just a smile. Trask wondered when his humanity had deserted him. When he had become little better than a cold-blooded drifter unable to do anything resembling a good deed. Slapping the long reins across the backs of the team he turned his head slightly so that he could watch her without her knowing. Watching her with eyes that had seen far more summers than her own, he knew that she required help. His help.

Trask knew he was going to help her, not for glory or for bags of gold, but for the good feeling it would bring him. It had been a long time since he had felt good, and he wanted to experience that emotion again. Even if it were for the last time.

2

The ride into the small town of no more than twenty buildings had taken over an hour. Trask had allowed the nervous team to take their time fearing they might spook again. He was no expert with anything with wheels. Sitting on the high plank of the buckboard was a new experience for him and one which he disliked. Trask preferred a sixteen hands high horse under his pants and anything else required skills he had never perfected. Entering the neat well-kept town he noted the small carefully painted sign which told him that this was Coffeeville.

Juliette Hart had not spoken since they had started their journey. Her blue eyes had been distant as they stared ahead during the trip. Staring but seeing nothing. Immersed in her own sorrow. Trask had steered the buck-board after tying his chestnut stallion to the tailgate and felt an unease in his bones he knew only too well. He instinctively knew that when murder visits the innocent, it leaves a trail of unanswered questions drowning in a sea of salty tears. The look upon her face was the same as that on hundreds of faces he had seen in the past: mothers looking at dead sons; daughters wailing over dead brothers. The look was always the same. A look that Trask knew only God had the answer for. No mortal man could understand how or why a loved one could cope with death when it reared its ugly head. Trask, like all men in his situation, could do little but watch and pity.

It seemed to him that everyone who dwelled in this small pleasant town was watching as he drove the sorrels into the centre of the main street. Pulling hard on the reins and setting the brake pole, Trask wrapped the long leathers around it until he was sure it was secure.

For several moments nothing happened as the observers kept a respectful distance. It was only when Trask stood and stepped onto the flat bed and removed his coat from the body that the townsfolk ventured closer. Soon the buckboard was surrounded by most of the town's residents. Faces went pale at the sight of the old man with the knife handle sticking from his back. Whispering turned into mumbling that soon verged on hysteria.

Trask dropped down onto the ground, and pushed his way through the gathering and moved around the front of the matched sorrels before standing beside the front passenger wheel below the white-faced female. She seemed to be unaware of where they were as he raised both his arms up to the silent Juliette. For a moment she remained motionless, then she turned and looked down into his face. Trask thought that he saw a hint in her eyes that she trusted him. Somehow she managed to allow him to assist her descent to the dusty street. She was helpless as he wrapped his arm around her shoulder protectively. Trask could hear gasps from the townswomen as they saw the bloodstained front of Juliette Hart's dress.

'This town got such a thing as a doctor?' Trask asked the crowd. There was no answer that was audible but the crowd seemed to breeze the pair across the street to a small wooden building. The sign outside the small white picket fence read, Joseph Vale MD.

It was a tired Trask who led the young, shocked female inside the building as the majority of the towns-men and women waited by the gate as if in silent vigil. It seemed that nearly the entire population of Coffeeville was standing outside the doctor's small house with two exceptions: two men remained beside the chestnut stallion that was tied to the tailgate of the buckboard.

The first was a well-dressed man with a moustache who chewed on a thin cigar allowing the smoke to drift up into his face The other was a burly man dressed in work clothes wearing a well-used Stetson. Pulling hard on the cigar and holding the smoke inside his thin chest before blowing it out deliberately the first man leaned over his companion's shoulder.

'Where the hell did this critter come from?' the smarter man asked his friend quietly.

'I ain't got no idea, Mr Davis.' The rougher of the pair shook his head in a confused manner. 'He wasn't around when I done for old man Hart.'

Giles Davis stared at his paid confederate from beneath the brim of his hat as he puffed feverishly on the thin cigar, blowing grey smoke through his clenched teeth.

'Any idea who he is? I can't say I recognize him.'

Dabs Carver shrugged. 'Nope. I ain't seen him before.'

Both men seemed unable to get to grips with the fact that their plans had been sabotaged by an unknown stranger. Neither would admit the fear that was filling both their hearts if indeed they had hearts beneath their contrasting outfits.

Just then the neater of the pair raised a finger and indicated the saddle horn where the gun-belt hung with its pair of Eagle-Butt Peacemakers in their holsters. 'Does that strike you as a little odd, Carver?'

'What, Mr Davis?'

'A man with such an exp shooting rig leaving them hang his saddle?' Davis stepped forward and looked at th more closely. His eyes w read the name that was h hand-tooled leather. 'C

Carver edged to 'What's the matter

'Read that,' D turning away a sidewalk.

'Trask!' Carver said aloud as he turned to look at his partner with an expression of disbelief written across his unshaven face. 'That must be Trask who just drove this rig in here Mr Davis.'

'I've heard of him.' Giles Davis sucked on his smoke and indicated for his friend to follow him down the street. The two men hurried as if their lives depended upon a fast getaway. They did not stop until they had entered the assayer's office. Davis closed the door and locked it. Turning to the smaller man he shook his head as f in total amazement. 'What I've heard n't very good from our point of view.'

'Is he trouble?'

No need to fret.' Davis blew a line of smoke at the floor as he took a of whiskey and two glasses off a 'We can handle him if he pokes into our business.'

t does it mean, Mr Davis? Why here?' The voice of Dabs d a fear in it that shook down

to his very boots. He, too, had heard the name Trask over the years and it was not a name that gave him any confidence.

Giles Davis removed his hat and tossed it onto the desk before pulling down the shades. The whiskey tasted good but was not good enough to take away the taste that fouled Davis's mouth. 'That's a good question, Carver. Why is Trask here? Wish the hell that I knew what the damn answer was.'

3

The late afternoon sun was hotter than hell itself as it burned down onto Trask's neck as he leaned against the picket fence rolling a cigarette. The crowd had filtered away an hour earlier and taken the body of the old man with them to the small funeral parlour at the very end of the street. Juliette Hart was lying on a cot inside the doctor's house after being given a sleeping draught that would enable her to sleep without being haunted by horrific nightmares. Eyes still watched him as his tongue ran across the white gum of the cigarette paper, eyes that hid in darkened doorways and from behind lace drapes, eyes that wondered who this strange man was as he struck a match and put its flame to the dry tobacco tip.

Drawing in the smoke, Trask watched with experienced eyes that had seen many things over his years of travelling through this big land. Trask would never allow those who watched him to become aware that he was also studying them. Standing away from the white fence he took in the neat buildings with their freshly painted façades. He had been to many places but never to such a clean town as Coffeeville.

He had two dollars in his jacket pocket and that should be lying on the flat bed of the buckboard, he thought. His paced footsteps took him across the wide street towards the pair of sorrels that were still standing where he had left them on arriving in this small town. Moving along to the rear of the flat bed and the lowered tailgate, Trask pulled the jacket off the dried blood.

His fingers found the two silver coins which he pushed into the back pocket of his jeans before staring at the soiled garment that had soaked up so much of the old man's blood. He tossed it back onto the buckboard as if unable to consider wearing it again in that condition. He had seen plenty of blood before over the last two decades but somehow this dark crimson soiling repulsed him.

Trask stood looking at his large chestnut still standing in his covering of grime and lather. Untying the reins, he led the stallion away from the buckboard and started to walk down towards the far end of the street where the brightest livery stable his eyes had ever seen stood with its massive red and white doors wide open.

The walk took him past a dozen or more buildings, some with small gardens filled with flowers and trees. He had never seen such a place before and it worried him. Towns were usually places where dirt gathered in human form but Coffeeville was the exception to the rule.

The long warm walk through the sunshine to the stables gave him cause to study the place well as he moved outside the large doors of the imposing building. Before he had even reached the livery, a large well-muscled man stepped out from the shadows and looked down on Trask.

'You want me to tend your horse, stranger?'

Trask thought about the two coins in his back pocket. 'How much is it gonna cost me, friend? I'm a bit short on cash.'

The man smiled and stepped up to the chestnut stallion and rubbed his hand over the white flame marking that ran down the centre of the creature's nose. 'Ain't gonna cost you a dime.'

Unused to generosity or charity, Trask rubbed his chin as he looked hard up at the tall man's face. 'Say that again?'

'I ain't gonna charge you nothing,' the man repeated.

Trask gave the reins to the livery man. 'How come?'

The big man led the chestnut into the cool of the large stable building as Trask followed behind still rubbing his chin and still smoking the thin ciga-rette. 'You brought little Juliette Hart safe into town, didn't you?'

'Yep.' Trask dropped the smoke at his feet and stepped on it, turning his boot sole hard to extinguish it.

Wrapping the reins around a stall booth upright the big stableman turned and stared at the fancy rig that hung from the saddle horn. 'I never seen a man with such a professional pair of guns who lets his horse wear them.'

Trask took the gun-belt from the large man and slung it over his shoulder. 'You sure you don't want paying?'

'I'm sure,' the big man said, throwing the Winchester into Trask's hands. 'What they call you stranger?'

'Trask.'

'I'm Joe. Joe Cooper.' The stableman reached down and pulled at the cinch strap before hauling the saddle from the animal's back and placing it onto the floor at his feet. The stallion seemed to immediately relax as the weight was taken from its spine. 'I'll look after this fine stallion, Trask. He's a beauty. He got a name to match his looks?'

'I just call him Smoke,' Trask replied.

'Smoke?' Cooper grinned. 'I'll take care of him real good.'

Trask paused as he reached the large doorway. 'Thanks, Joe.'

Cooper watched as Trask headed out into the sun carrying his weapons. He had never heard the name of Trask before. To him it was meaningless.

4

The saloon was unlike any Trask had ever entered before. It was clean, free of sawdust and lacked a single female. The thought of there being women of the night in Coffeeville was an outrageous idea and made the mature man smile as he approached the bar where an elderly man stood waiting. Trask gave the man a nod as he rested the carbine onto the counter.

'What'll it be, stranger?' the old man asked, looking as if he could not pull a cork out of a bottle without assistance.

'A beer and some information,' Trask replied.

The beer came slow but not nearly as slow as the next words from the old man. 'What you mean by information? Do I look the sort that knows anything about anything stranger?'

Trask accepted the glass and placed

one of his silver dollars onto the counter. 'Thanks. And you look to me as if you know quite a bit.'

'When you've lived as long as me, you tend to forget more than you remember, sonny.' The bartender pushed the money back towards Trask. 'You ain't paying for no drinks in my saloon.'

Once again Trask felt surprise rush over him as he sipped the cold beer. His eyes looked up into the mirror behind the old man as he watched the two men entering behind him. Instantly Trask felt a cold shudder racing up his spine. It was the first time since entering this small quaint town that he had sensed danger.

Turning with the beer in one hand and his buckled gun-belt hanging over his shoulder, he stared at the ill-matched pair as they approached him.

'Howdy, Trask,' Giles Davis said as he and Dabs Carver reached him.

It was a strange expression that Trask cast upon the two men as he finished his beer. 'You know me, mister?'

'Who doesn't know the legendary Trask?' Davis sighed, as Carver weighed up the man who was placing his empty glass on the bar.

'The question is, how the hell do you know the 'legendary Trask', mister?' Trask looked the pair up and down carefully as if they were vipers ready to strike at him with poisonous fangs. His expression was void of anything that might allow his thoughts to be anticipated.

Dabs Carver had been unable to take his eyes from Trask since the two men had entered the saloon. His was a keenness to tempt fate. 'I've heard tell that you are mighty good with them irons of yours.'

Trask glanced from under the brim of his hat, as he had done a hundred times before in different saloons at different men with loud voices. 'And you are?'

'My name's Dabs Carver.'

'I never heard a thing about you,' Trask said coldly. 'Maybe you ain't done nothing?'

'I done plenty, old man.' Carver moved forward angrily before Davis stepped between the two men who were eyeing each other up carefully.

'Steady, Carver. I would hate for you to get yourself gunned down before payday.' Giles Davis tried to make his hostile hired gun calm down. 'Easy.'

'You listen to the man, Carver,' Trask advised. 'Take it easy and you just might live longer.'

The smiling Davis moved closer to the bar and dropped a coin on top. 'My usual, gramps.'

The bartender lifted a bottle of rye and placed it in front of the smartly dressed man. 'Usual it is, Mr Davis.'

'Davis?' Trask looked the man up and down. He had never seen anyone quite so clean before. 'You still ain't told me how you know who I am.'

'I saw the name on your gun-belt earlier,' Davis answered pouring himself a glassful of the brown liquor. 'Simple as that.'

Trask nodded. 'Why you need the monkey?' He pointed at Carver and started to grin.

Carver's face suddenly turned bright red under the grime of sheer neglect. 'What he call me, Mr Davis?'

'Quiet, Carver,' Davis snapped as he downed his drink. He had not met many men like Trask, but had expected something more, far more flamboyant. Looking at the man who seemed to be covered from his Stetson down to his boots in caked dust, was not what Davis had expected. There was more than a little disappointment in the dude's face as he refilled his glass. 'Trask here just wants a quiet time. No need to hassle the gent.'

'He ain't calling you names, Mr Davis.' Carver stepped a little closer to the man with his gun-belt hanging over his shoulder and spat at his feet. 'You look burned out to me, Trask. You look like an old man who ain't got nothing left except a reputation.'

The smile on Trask's face grew wider

as he glanced at the bartender. 'Another beer, barkeep.'

Davis's eyes narrowed as he watched his hired gun getting an itchy trigger-finger. He knew that there was nothing he could do now. Carver was just too angry to reason with. Looking at the figure of Trask as he stood motionless, he began to wonder if Carver's words might not be close to the mark. Trask looked nothing like a gunfighter standing wearily at the bar. The man didn't even have the sense to strap on his guns.

Dabs Carver squared up to Trask and hovered his hand over the gun grip of his pistol. 'Let's see if you are as fast as they say you are, Trask.'

Trask turned and took the glass of cold beer from the elderly bartender and sipped the beverage slowly. Lowering the glass, he stared at Carver with eyes that had out-stared a hundred men in a hundred saloons. 'Why not go for that pistol of yours, Carver? Let me see if you are as fast as you seem to think you are.'

Davis lifted his bottle and stepped two paces away from Trask as if expecting his man to shoot wide of the target and not wishing to get plugged by a bullet that he had paid for.

It was Dabs Carver's move. It was his play. Trask was standing drinking his beer calmly with his guns in their holsters hanging on the expensive belt over his broad shoulder. Carver had never faced a man with such a cold stare before, but then, he seldom faced his victims. He preferred to attack from behind when the victim was not expecting anything.

Trask lowered his glass from his lips again. 'Make your play, sonny, or maybe you just can't cut it?'

Carver could not resist the target any longer. He went for his gun as fast as he could.

Just as the weapon had cleared its holster, Trask tossed the remnants of his beer into the younger man's face and stepped forward. Kicking the wet-faced man as hard as he could in the middle, he waited for the winded head to drop before kneeing the man's jaw. Carver fell unconscious at his feet still holding the Colt as blood dribbled from his mouth.

Davis gasped and then poured himself another whiskey. 'Phew, that was slick, Trask.'

'How much do you pay him, Davis?' Trask asked, handing his empty glass to the bartender to be refilled.

'Twenty a month and found,' Davis replied.

'That seems a mite too much,' Trask remarked as his eyes studied the prone Carver on the floor. 'Hotheads make me angry.'

'I agree with you, Trask.' Davis felt a shiver rushing up his spine beneath his expensive shirt.

'I have run into hundreds of the snot-nosed bums in my time and they always end up the same way.' Trask watched the smart man as a bead of sweat trickled from under the hat brim down across his face.

'Dead?'

'For the most part.' Trask rested his elbows on the bar, as his eyes stayed aimed at the man at his feet. 'Why do folks like you hire trash like Carver?'

Davis cleared his throat and nodded in agreement. 'I reckon if a man like me was able to hire a man like your-self . . . '

'I ain't for hire,' Trask said coldly.

There was something about Dabs Carver that did not sit right in Trask's mind yet he could not work out what it was. Bending down he took the gun from the unconscious man's hand and opened the chamber allowing the bullets to cascade onto the floor. Then he held out the empty Colt to Giles Davis who reluctantly accepted it. 'Don't let him load this if he's still thinking of coming to test me, Davis.'

Davis swallowed. 'I could sure use a man like you, Trask.'

'I ain't for hire,' Trask repeated.

'I'll pay you a hundred a month.'

Trask looked the dude up and down curiously. 'A hundred dollars a month?'

Davis sipped at his whiskey never taking his eyes from the thoughtful gunfighter. 'Interested?'

Trask finished his beer and picked up his Winchester off the bar top. He stepped over Carver and then continued to the swing doors. Pushing one of the doors ajar he paused and turned to look at Davis hard. 'I'll think about it, Davis.'

Giles Davis watched the swing door swaying back and forth as Trask disappeared out into the late afternoon sunshine. Whatever the gunfighter was, he thought, he was not a man to break under pressure nor give in to temptation. Trask was certainly a man who could handle himself as he had proven with Carver, yet could he still use those impressive Peacemakers?

No man could have lived as long as the grey-haired Trask without some degree of speed with his weaponry, surely? Davis swallowed his whiskey

43

and gave the bottle back to the bartender before kneeling beside the man with a mouth filled with his own blood and cracked teeth. Davis started to slap Carver's face trying to wake his hired gun. With every slap he started to wonder if he was paying Carver far more than he was worth.

★ ★ ★

Trask stared up and down the small street for more than five minutes before suddenly realizing what was bothering him. There was no sign of a sheriff's office anywhere. Could this beautiful place be devoid of law? Trask walked across the street into the long shadows and gazed up and down from another angle. If there was law in Coffeeville, he certainly couldn't see it. Then as the powerfully built Joe Cooper ambled from the livery stables towards him, Trask headed the man off.

'Howdy again, Trask,' Cooper said, as he strode towards Juliette Hart's buckboard. 'Come to help me take the team up to the livery?'

Trask had nothing else to do. 'Why not, Joe? Why not.'

The two men unhitched the team of matched sorrels and led them back in the direction of the red and white stables. With one horse each it was a quick and simple operation. With the two horses rubbed down and released into the large paddock at the side of the massive wooden building, the two men relaxed. Using hay bales as seats the two faced each other thoughtfully.

'What's eating at you, Trask?' Cooper asked.

'This town, I guess,' came the honest reply.

'Coffeeville? How come?'

'Has this town got any law?' Trask brought out the small bag of tobacco and pulled out a slim paper and began sprinkling the golden leaf carefully.

'Never needed any law in Coffeeville,' Cooper answered as he watched the man making his smoke.

'Until today,' Trask said looking up as he licked the gummed paper.

'Yep. Until today.' Cooper seemed to be curious about the small tobacco pouch. 'Can I have a try?'

Trask handed the pouch over to the man with huge fingers as he struck a match and lit his cigarette. 'So this place is always peaceful?'

'Nope.' Cooper shook his head as he carefully poured the fine tobacco along the paper and then hung the pouch by its draw string on his teeth. 'A few strange things been happening over the past few months though. Things that have started to make folks a mite scared.'

Trask inhaled. 'What kinda things?'

'Murders,' Cooper said as he ran his tongue along the gum and somehow managed to get a mouthful of tobacco.

'How many murders, Joe?'

'Three before today.' The stableman spat out the weed and tossed the pouch back into Trask's hands. 'We ain't wanted the law to come in from outside and ruin our valley, but things are getting a tad ugly.'

Blowing out a long line of smoke, Trask offered the cigarette to the larger man who accepted it happily. 'Juliette Hart's father the only man to get a knife in his back?'

'Tom Hart was pretty good to me over the years. To get a knife in the back isn't right.' Cooper smacked a fist into the palm of his other hand. 'The other three farmers all got killed differently. One was shot; one broke his neck in a fall, and the other had his brains smashed in by a rockfall.'

'Apart from the man who was shot, the other two sound like accidents.' Trask accepted his smoke back and took the final lungful of smoke before crushing it under his boot. 'How come you say that they were murdered Joe?'

Joe Cooper nodded at the man. 'You seen rockfall victims?'

'Nope.'

'I have. The farmer who was found

underneath them boulders had been dead before the rocks hit him.' Cooper seemed to know what he was talking about. 'I tell you them farmers were murdered.'

Trask believed the bigger man. 'Tom Hart was also a farmer?'

'They have all been farmers.' Cooper raised an eyebrow. 'Is that a mite fishy?'

'Kinda fishy, Joe,' Trask admitted, getting to his feet and moving to the open doorway of the livery stable. Leaning on the wooden wall he stared at the brightly painted street. The sight of so many well-cared-for properties had fooled his weary eyes into thinking that he had arrived somewhere special, a place where the evil of the outside world had not truly touched. Staring at the orange sunlight as it traced its way over the buildings, Trask knew that he had been mistaken. Evil had touched this place.

'Where you staying tonight, Trask?' Cooper asked, rising to his feet.

'Is there a hotel or boarding-house in

Coffeeville?' Trask looked up into the man's face.

Cooper shook his head. 'Nope. There ain't no call. We don't get many folks passing through.'

'Then I guess I might be camping under the stars tonight, Joe.' Trask was used to having the ground as his mattress and the stars as his ceiling.

'You could stay with me.' The big man pointed to the side of the livery where a small wooden building stood, a solid structure made by his own strong hands. 'I got plenty of room.'

Trask smiled and patted the man on the muscular shoulder in gratitude. 'Thanks, Joe.'

Cooper picked up the Winchester off the ground. 'I'll take this into the house and get the stove lit. I reckon we both could use some grub.'

The gunfighter slowly picked up his gun-belt from the bale of hay and hung it over his shoulder. 'I'm gonna check on Juliette Hart. I'm gonna ask the doctor when she'll be able to leave town.'

'You like her, Trask?' Cooper grinned.

'I've seen a lot worse.'

'I've shod a lot worse.'

'Get that stove lit, Joe,' Trask smiled.

Cooper watched as the man strode out into the dying rays of the sun carrying the impressive shooting rig over his shoulder as usual. The stableman wondered why Trask did not simply strap it on around his middle as lesser skilled men did. It seemed as if Trask could not bring himself to do so, as if the guns made him uneasy. Cooper shook his head and walked to his small house with Trask's carbine gripped in his large fist.

Whatever the reason for the gun-fighter's unusual behaviour the large muscular man knew that he might never learn the real answer. Cooper opened the door to his house and watched as Trask went through the picket fence and towards the front door of the doctor's. Trask was a good man, he thought.

★ ★ ★

It was dark as Trask left the quiet of the doctor's home and paced to the gate. The street only had three oil-filled street lamps on ten-foot tall poles. Their light was barely enough to highlight anything as most of their glowing seemed to be lost in the leaves of the dozens of carefully trimmed trees. Trask hesitated as he closed the gate behind him and pondered upon the doctor's words. The young Juliette was recovering and had eaten earlier, but had still to regain the gift of speech. Trask knew by experience that shock affected folks in differing ways. Grief might be a burden but shock was dangerous. The mature man gazed down the quiet street at the glowing lights from behind window drapes. Only the saloon still showed any sign of life as its light cast out onto the street through the swing doors.

Touching the gun-belt as it hung over his broad shoulder he aimed his pointed boots at the small house that was tacked onto the side of the livery stable.

Trask found himself instinctively ducking as the bright flashes traced across from out of the darkness at him. It was like watching crazed lightning bugs as the red-hot lead passed above him. A split second later the deafening sound of gunfire echoed around the small street as its sounds bounced off the solid buildings.

Trask crawled to a broad tree and swiftly found the pair of eagle butts in his hands. He returned the fire as he saw another bright flash from the distant corner of the assayer's office. His shots were high and clipped the edge brickwork off the corner which sat within the darkness.

Moving with his head low, Trask ran across the street until he found another tree to rest his spine against. Lifting his weapons again he saw two more flashes emanating from the dark alley. Trask felt his hands raise and his fingers squeezing the triggers. Two blasts from his guns and a distant shriek followed by the clatter of a water barrel being forced over under the weight of an injured man filled his ears. Trask ran at the sound with his pistols jutting out from his wrists. Within ten paces of the injured man, Trask recognized the figure lying in the darkness as the lamplight opposite glinted off his gun.

Seeing the gun move as he rapidly approached, Trask blasted two more bullets into the prone figure of Dabs Carver.

Carver's body arched in an almost theatrical manner as life left him to be replaced by the suddenness of death. The gasp seemed to hiss from the man's mouth as the body sank into the ground at Trask's feet.

The keen senses of the man with the eagle-butt Peacemakers in his hands were aware that another man had made a quick departure through the black shadows between the buildings. Cautiously, a few figures appeared from the safety of their homes and the bright saloon. Trask said nothing to them as they took in the situation and figured it out themselves.

'You OK, Trask?' Cooper asked from the centre of the dark street.

Trask looked away from the death he had created at the big man who stood holding his discarded gun-belt in his hands. Moving towards the man he nodded as they both headed back in the direction of the stables.

'Who was that?' Cooper asked, as Trask accepted the leather belt and slid the two pistols into their holsters.

'Carver,' Trask replied as he held the belt at arm's length so that it almost touched the ground as they walked.

'He try to bushwhack you?'

'He did,' Trask replied as they went inside the small house filled with the smell of cooking.

Cooper closed the door and slid the wooden bolt across before returning to the stove and replacing the pan filled with salt bacon over the flames. 'Why would Carver try and kill you?'

Trask placed the gun-belt on the chair before seating himself and sighing. 'I figure I am in some varmint's way, Joe.'

'Carver worked for Davis, the assayer.'

'Exactly.'

5

Sunrise came early in the quiet valley. Its orange glow danced down over the trees until it covered every leaf of every tree and every building in Coffeeville.

There was a silence in the streets that only a couple of roosters defied. When Joe Cooper opened his weary eyes he saw the troubled figure of Trask standing beside the window staring blankly out at the town.

'Did I wake you, Joe?' Trask asked over his shoulder as the big man swung his legs over the edge of the cot.

'Nope. I usually get up at dawn,' Cooper gruffed trying to find his socks amongst the litter on the floor between the two bunks.

'Sorry.' Trask gazed out at the empty street through the grimy window panes.

'That shooting eating at you?' Cooper shook the dust from his sock before pulling it over his foot.

'Nope.' Trask turned and moved back to his cot and sat down opposite the bigger man. 'I just don't like the way things are panning out.'

'Whatcha mean?'

'Something is gnawing at my craw, Joe.' Trask rubbed his face feeling the whiskers. 'There's trouble brewing in this beautiful valley. Bad trouble.'

Cooper stared hard at the man as he rubbed the sleep from the corners of his eyes. 'Reckon?'

'I reckon.'

'What ya gonna do?'

'If you've a straight razor, I'm gonna shave.'

Cooper pointed at the shelf. 'Big trouble for Miss Juliette?'

'I think there are a few other folks who are in just as much danger, Joe,' Trask said thoughtfully.

'Who?'

Trask rose to his feet and plucked the razor off the shelf and opened the blade. His eyes studied the honed edge.

'I better find out fast otherwise I can't help them.'

No more words passed between the two men for another hour as both considered what they knew and worried about what they did not know.

* * *

Coffeeville had no structure like average towns. Without lawmen or even a town council it was just a gathering of buildings set in the heart of a valley. Having no leaders it simply existed as it had always done, a place where like minded folks gathered and lived. A place where time seemed to stand still. In normal circumstances, this would have been Utopia but for Trask as he tried to gain some general consensus amongst the population, it was more of a nightmare.

The clock in the saloon struck eleven as Trask entered and made his way up to the bar. Cooper stayed close at his side as they made their way through the dozen or so men. Trask required the full backing of each and every citizen of Coffeeville if he was to act to prevent further killings.

Every eye was on the gunfighter who rested a foot on the brass rail around the bar. Trask turned and knew that he had their attention, now he had to use it.

'You this Trask fella?' Matt Hume, the local butcher asked from the front of the crowd.

Trask nodded. 'That's what they call me.'

'How come you don't strap on that gun-belt?' Bert Hartnell the owner of the small bakery enquired. 'Instead of walking around with it hanging over your dang shoulder?'

'T'ain't natural,' another voice chipped in.

Trask looked at Cooper and smiled. 'They seem a nice friendly bunch of critters, Joe.'

Cooper tossed a coin onto the bar and watched as the old bartender started

59

to fill two glasses with beer. 'They can be real lively if ya catch them right.'

'You folks don't know me,' Trask began. 'All I can say is that I'm here to help you folks.'

'Help us?' Jack Smith the barber raised an eyebrow. 'Was killing Dabs Carver the kinda help we need?'

Trask placed his gun-belt upon the bar and rested his elbows against the cold wood. 'Carver opened up on me and I just finished what he had so stupidly begun, mister.'

'You often kill folks, Trask?' the butcher asked coldly, staring at the man before him.

'I have never killed anyone who wasn't trying to kill me first if that's what you mean.' Trask cast his eyes across the faces of the men. He knew that they were a decent lot but troubled as he himself was troubled.

'You ain't answered the question about your guns.'

'How come you don't strap them on?'

Trask looked down at his feet before answering. 'Sometimes a man can become the slave of his weapons. I only strap them on when I have to do so.'

'Trask is trying to help us, boys,' Joe Cooper said loudly, as he rested his beer glass down on the bar counter. 'Stop acting like a bunch of old hens.'

The gathered men knew that the big stableman seldom gave anyone a kind word, and if he trusted the stranger it might just be in their favour to do likewise. There was a sudden hush as the men began to take seats in front of Trask. Suddenly, they were listening.

Cooper nodded as Trask smiled in his direction before turning back to the dozen men.

'Joe here tells me that Thomas Hart wasn't the first to get himself killed in this valley,' Trask began. 'Last night Carver tried to bushwhack me for some reason. I've a feeling that there are a few others at risk in this valley.'

'At risk from whom?' The familiar

61

voice of Giles Davis was loud and strong as it echoed around the saloon.

The seated townsmen turned and stared at the swing doors as the assayer strolled in. Trask stood upright and screwed up his eyes at the man who walked purposely towards him.

'Trask,' Davis said, touching the brim of his hat as he reached the bar and tossed a coin at the bartender. 'My usual, gramps.'

It was a confused Trask who turned to face the elegant man standing beside him. 'Davis,' he acknowledged.

'You stirring up the townspeople Trask?' Davis lifted his glass to his lips and sipped at his drink. 'I thought you were a tough gunfighter, not a man who sees demons.'

'Your boy Carver tried to bushwhack me last night,' Trask whispered into the man's ear. 'I guess you don't know anything about it. Right?'

'Correct, Trask.' Davis glanced across at the weathered face of the gunfighter. 'I fired Carver after you beat him up yesterday. I guess he just had a grudge against you and decided to try and get even.'

Trask grinned. 'Convenient, Davis. A mite convenient.'

Davis shrugged. 'The truth is you seem to be looking for something that doesn't exist, Trask. Why not leave these folks to go about their lives?'

'So you had nothing to do with Carver's actions, Davis?'

Giles Davis finished his drink and placed the glass down so that it could be refilled. 'You think I want to do you harm? I am just a peace-loving assayer, Trask. Nothing more.'

Cooper rested a hand on Trask's shoulder. 'Come on, Trask.'

Trask picked up his gun-belt and placed it over his shoulder before following the big man from the saloon. Once out on the sidewalk he took a deep breath.

'Give that man enough rope and he might just hang himself,' Joe Cooper said quietly.

'Giles Davis has sure got some brass, Joe.'

'It's lead that counts, Trask,' Cooper said in a low cogent tone. 'You have the edge on him in that department.'

'Backshooters always have the edge, Joe.'

'Come on. We'll get some grub before checking on Miss Juliette.'

Trask bit his bottom lip and followed Cooper down the street towards the livery.

6

Four men stood side by side at the saloon bar in the township of Fairfax, four hard-drinking, hard-talking men. Men who barely knew the difference between right or wrong and whose only master was the coin their services purchased. Never had these four gunmen ever concerned themselves as to the morals of their deeds. The price had been paid and the quartet were drinking to their new job before mounting up and heading for the remote town in the strange valley known as Coffeeville.

Todd Fern was the self-appointed leader of the four ruthless hired gunfighters. A tall man of dubious character and amazing skill with his Colts. The three smaller men were all in their early twenties and had little hope of reaching their third decade as long as they continued in their present occupation. Jeff Leeming was the loudest of the group and a skilled man with both handgun and repeating rifle. An army deserter, he had found himself accepted into this small band easily. The widest of the four was called simply Tubbs. A man who had an enormous appetite for killing and food. Tubbs seemed unable to do anything by half measures but that was his only weakness. The last man at the bar drinking his rot-gut whiskey was called Sonny Evans. A quiet sort who was equally as dangerous as any of the other men but stayed silent most of the time. Evans drank and listened. To him, the sheer fun of the game was why he rode with these three other misfits. He enjoyed the life of a hired gun and all its extras that could be taken. Evans might have been the quietest of the bunch but he was just as evil as any of his comrades. To him, it was just a game. Killing meant nothing to him as he had been doing it for far too many years. It was now a habit. And habits are damn hard to shake when you enjoy them.

Todd Fern held the scrap of paper in his grubby hand as his men drank beside him. A telegraph message that he had been expecting for weeks, and was pleased that it had finally arrived. The wire was from Giles Davis. Its simple message read:

BRING MEN. YOUR SERVICES ARE NOW NEEDED. FIVE HUNDRED DOLLARS. SIGNED DAVIS.

Davis had ridden forty miles to send that wire to Fern. Fern had worked for the assayer before and knew that when Davis promised a fee, it would be paid in two instalments Half up front and half upon completion. The faster Fern and his boys got the job done, the faster they would receive the second part of their fee.

'What we gotta do this time, Todd?' Tubbs asked, grabbing the remainder of the bread set out before them next to the tall clear glass bottles.

Fern watched as the fat man filled his mouth with the food before replying, 'Same as always, Tubbs. We gotta kill.'

Leeming leaned over the taller man and gave the paper a glance as if he were capable of reading it. 'How many we gotta kill?'

Todd Fern gave the fat man another look as he choked on the bread rather than allow his friends to share the meal, before turning his eyes down into Leeming's face. 'Davis will fill in the details when we get there, Jeff.'

'I ain't been to Coffeeville before,' Leeming said thinking about the earlier conversation that had filled the saloon air when Fern had announced the wire to them. 'Is it a big town?'

Fern shook his head as he lifted his glass and swallowed the rough whiskey. 'I couldn't say. All I know about the place is that it's in the heart of a valley. A valley that nobody ever named and is filled with farms and farmers.'

Sonny Evans suddenly looked interested. 'Farms?'

'Yep.' Fern nodded.

The youthful features of Evans grinned as he thought about farms and farmers. 'Them farmers usually got daughters.'

Fern watched as the man drooled into his glass. 'Reckon so, Sonny.'

The four men continued to drink until Todd Fern knew that it was time to get out of the smoke-filled saloon and get on their waiting horses. The people who watched the four trail-hardened men as they mounted their horses in the windswept street were the sort who knew trouble when they saw it. To see it stepping into stirrups and riding away brought relief.

Fern led the strange bunch of riders out of the small town and headed east. He knew how to find the valley and therefore, find Coffeeville.

The strange riders left nobody regretting their leaving in the township of Fairfax. Sometimes even the greedy saloon owners have to admit that some folks are better riding out of town rather than riding into it. As the four riders finally disappeared from sight the entire town breathed a sigh of relief. They were gone and soon they would be someone else's problem. The citizens of Coffeeville and the people who dwelled in the nameless valley had no idea the trouble that was riding toward them. With the exception of Giles Davis that is. Only he knew they were coming; only he knew why he had sent for them.

★ ★ ★

'Where you headed, Trask?' Joe Cooper asked, as he watched the quiet man step into his stirrup and hoist himself into his saddle slowly. Trask said nothing for a moment as he buckled his gun-belt and hung it over the saddle horn. Then his face changed as if a thought had drifted into his mind. No simple thought. No idle thought.

'Where you headed?' Cooper repeated, looking up at the man holding the reins firmly as he checked himself in the saddle.

'I'm gonna take me a ride around this big old green valley of yours, Joe,' Trask answered.

'What the hell for?' The big man watched the face of the mature man as he slid the Winchester scabbard under his saddle until it would go no further.

'Answers, Joe.' Trask rode out into the sunlight through the wide doors of the stable before easing his horse to a halt. 'I've been asking a lot of questions when I should have been looking for the answers.'

Cooper scratched his head. 'Nope. I still don't get it, Trask.'

'Neither do I.' Trask pulled his Stetson down to shield his eyes from the sun. 'But I intend trying to figure all this out. So I reckon I'll start at the beginning. Where does Giles Davis live, Joe?'

'He's got a farm about two miles east

of here,' Cooper answered. 'Not that he's any farmer. What do you wanna go and see his place for?'

Trask did not reply. He simply drove his horse in the direction that Cooper's large arm had indicated. There was a confidence in the way Trask rode his horse that echoed of his earlier days when the creeping vulture called Father Time, had not laid claim upon his ageing body. The big man watched as the dust drifted in the afternoon breeze until the rider was out of sight.

7

Trask pulled hard on his reins and slowed Smoke to a stop on the crest of a low, tree-lined ridge. Trees filled the area making long cooling shadows for the rider. Trask had found what he had been seeking for the past hour. Ahead of him he watched the house that was anything but small. Trask had never seen such a house and wondered how and why Giles Davis required such a lavish property just to sleep in.

Trask had never owned a house of any size over the years and there was more than a little envy in his breast as he carefully studied the building from the dense trees. Then he heard the sound of a single horse-drawn buggy coming along the dirt road to his left from Coffeeville. He steadied his mount and watched as Davis drove the buggy into the wide gateway and up towards the house until he was out of sight.

Being a man of curious nature, Trask rode from the cover of the trees and galloped after the buggy at top speed. He had no idea why he was following the buggy up to the big house, but that did not stop his haste in catching up with the vehicle. He reached the house only seconds after Davis and reined in his horse hard as he saw the debonair man stepping from the small shining buggy. A small careworn servant took the black carriage to a huge barn as Giles Davis watched Trask bringing his horse to a final stop at the steps of the house.

Both men stared at each other momentarily. Davis noted that Trask still favoured hanging his gun-belt from the horn of his saddle rather than strapped around his hips like any normal man would do.

There was little in the way of kindness in Davis's voice as he spoke to the rider. 'So you are now coming here to my home, Trask.'

'Any reason why I shouldn't pay you a call?' Trask dismounted and walked up to the man.

'Is this a visit or is there something else on your mind?'

'Just a visit.' Trask gave the house another long hard look and could not disguise his admiration, not for its owner but for its builder. It was by far the most impressive edifice he had ever set eyes upon.

'Like my little home?' Giles Davis seemed to be gloating in his own superior wealth over the trail-hardened rider.

'Mighty fine place you got here,' Trask said truthfully as he removed his Stetson and beat the dust off against his leg. 'I ain't never seen one better and I've seen plenty.'

Davis could not allow flattery to go without the offer of a drink. 'Would you care to come inside and have yourself a long drink, Trask?'

Trask grinned wide as he followed Davis into the house through a dark stained door that was wider than any door he had ever seen on a house before. 'A cool drink would go down well and might just wash the flies off my teeth.'

As Davis led the way into a room filled with books and statues he looked over his shoulder at the dusty man in his wake. 'You thought about my offer of a job?'

Trask stopped and looked at the furniture as Davis poured two glasses of liquor from a crystal decanter. The chairs looked as though they might break under the weight of any normal man. They also looked too clean for anyone such as himself to sit upon. Trask hated things that were pretty and lacked practicality.

'Well?' Davis repeated. 'Do you want to work for me? I'm a man short since you killed Carver.'

'I ain't thought about hiring out to nobody,' Trask answered as he took the glass from Davis and sipped at the drink. It tasted expensive although he had no idea what it was. 'Carver was no loss to the world, Davis.'

'Why are you so damn adamant?'

Trask shrugged. 'I ain't a hired gunslinger, Davis. That sort are ten a penny and I ain't one of them.'

'But you are the famous Trask.' Davis carefully watched the face of the man and yet could see no sign of weakness displayed in any of the weathered lines that etched across his tanned skin.

'If I'm famous, it ain't for being a hired gun.' Trask finished his drink and placed the glass onto a table. 'Well, thanks for the drink, Davis. I'd better be on my way. I got me a lot to do.'

'Such as what?' Davis weighed the man up and yet could not break through the armour that protected him. Trask was wearing clothes that had seen far better days and looked desperately out of place in the lavish surroundings of Davis's home, yet he had left his weapons on the horse outside. This was not the action of the average gunfighter who never allowed his pistols or rifle to stray far from reach. Trask seemed to relish the idea of risking his safety by never strapping on his handsome gun-belt and that troubled the assayer.

Davis followed the confident man as he headed towards the front door and the bright afternoon sunlight. 'What did you come all the way out here for, Trask?'

Trask gathered his reins and held onto the saddle horn before mounting. As he raised the leathers in his hands he smiled down at the man about whom he felt so uneasy. 'Hell, Davis. Ain't you ever met a critter who is just plain nosy before?'

'I just can't accept that the famous Trask is nosy, friend,' Davis shrugged. 'It just doesn't figure.'

'Not much in my life has ever made sense.' Trask spurred his horse and headed towards the gate. 'I'll be seeing you again real soon, Mr Davis.'

Giles Davis watched silently as the rider galloped away from his home. Standing silently on the wide steps of his house he wondered about Trask and if he might be one large heap of trouble that could not be bought off. Trouble that would keep on coming when any normal man would back away. Would Trask ruin his plan? That was a question which was yet to be answered.

Whatever the reason for the mysterious Trask's interest, the normally cool-headed Giles Davis disliked the feeling in his guts and the smell of his own sweat as it trickled from beneath his arms and soiled his expensive shirt.

Trask was like a mink that had sunk its teeth into his flesh and would never let go whilst he still had life flowing through his veins.

8

It was a frail and fragile-looking Juliette Hart who was gently led from the sanctuary of the doctor's home just after nine in the morning. The horror that she had witnessed two days earlier still haunted her every waking second as she stepped along the small path to the white picket fence where Trask stood waiting. The women of Coffeeville had brought her a fine new dress to replace the blood-covered one she had arrived wearing. It was crisp and blue and suited her. Trask had her buckboard waiting with his horse tied securely to the tailgate. The blood had been scrubbed from the wooden planks of the vehicle during its stay at Cooper's livery and now smelled of strong carbolic soap. Her long dark eyelashes fluttered as she found herself focusing upon the man she recognized as having saved her.

Trask had arranged with the elderly Doc Vale that he would take her back to her farm and stay as long as she required. As long as he was fed and his horse grained, he knew that it would be time well spent. He still had two dollars sitting in his shirt pocket and yet felt a lot richer than most of the folks he had met in this strange valley. Trask had the wisdom of years in the saddle to help him whilst they had only the small world around them for reference. With vultures like Giles Davis hovering above their heads these people were almost helpless and it seemed only Trask recognized the danger.

'You will be fine with Trask, Miss Juliette,' Doc Vale said in a low comforting tone as he passed her small arm to the strong firm hands of the gunfighter. 'He will escort you home, dear. Go with him.'

'My father?' Her voice broke as she spoke. 'What of my poor father?'

Vale shook his head woefully. 'The

undertaker will arrange everything, girl. You must not concern yourself with such things. You are not well enough.'

'But . . . ' Her sentence faded as she felt the strength of the gentle hands of Trask on her arm. She looked hard at him and then found the first smile of this new day.

'Miss Hart.' Trask smiled as he assisted her slow careful climb up onto the high driving board of the buckboard. When he was satisfied she was safely seated he turned to the doctor who so discreetly handed him a box of sleeping-powders. Trask tucked them into his shirt and then buttoned himself up.

'Two powders tonight, Trask,' Vale advised. 'Then one every four hours until the box is empty.'

'What are these for, Doc?' Trask held little trust in medicines as he had never had call to use any himself.

'To allow her to rest and sleep,' Vale replied. 'Only sleep will help her gain the strength she requires.'

Trask nodded as he pulled his Stetson down over his eyes and bit his lip. 'Then she'll be OK?'

Vale nodded positively. 'Then she will be fine.'

As Trask watched the doctor moving back towards his house the sight of Joe Cooper loomed up in the corner of his eye as he approached carrying the infamous gun-belt with the name 'Trask' branded into its thick leather in one hand and the Winchester in the other.

'Joe,' Trask acknowledged, as he walked around the noses of the pair of matched horses that stood in the harness.

'You forgot to take these from my house this morning,' Cooper said firmly. 'You will end up losing these guns one day if you ain't careful.'

Trask took the gun-belt and stared at the beautiful guns in their holsters. 'These guns would never allow me to leave without them, Joe.'

Cooper looked puzzled. 'Stop kidding. You aiming to stay on the Hart farm looking after Miss Juliette?'

'I ain't got nothing better to do, Joe.' Trask tried not to think about the dangers that he knew lay ahead. 'The kid might just need my services as a gunfighter.'

'You reckon she's in danger?' Cooper asked in a lowered voice that only Trask could hear.

'Yep,' Trask said through gritted teeth. 'It ain't over, Joe. In fact I think it's only just beginning.'

Cooper looked at the guns thoughtfully. 'How come you seem to have such a strange way with them guns, Trask?'

'Because I think they are magic,' Trask winked, as he climbed up into the driver's position of the buckboard and placed the belt between himself and the quiet Juliette Hart.

Cooper handed the Winchester up into Trask's hands. 'Magic?'

Trask grinned as he lay the rifle at his feet in the box next to his left boot. 'Do you believe in magic, Joe?'

'I ain't sure, Trask.' Cooper scratched

his head as he watched the mysterious gunfighter release the brake pole and slap the long reins across the backs of the matched team. The buckboard headed slowly down the street of Coffeeville on its journey back to the Hart farm. Trask's eyes studied the assayer's office as he passed and knew that Davis was watching.

Trask got the team up to speed as they exited the town line and headed out into the fertile valley. The morning air tasted fresher than any air Trask had ever tasted before. There was a sweetness in it that was hard to define. Maybe it was because there were so many flowers edging the verge of the road that led into the deepest part of the valley. Maybe it was the mountain range that dominated the distant horizon allowing the snow and ice to cool the air making it taste fresher. Trask glanced over his curled gun-belt at the silent figure who just sat with her hands in her lap staring ahead. Maybe it was just the company, he thought.

* * *

The journey to the remote valley was no easy one but the four riders continued on their route. There was a lot of easy money waiting for them in Coffeeville and they wanted it. They needed it. Killing paid well, but when you drank like these men constantly drank, money soon disappeared. More money meant more killings. It was a vicious circle. A very bloody vicious circle.

There were few towns between them and the distant hidden valley but the four killers knew them all. The first town they avoided as they had stirred up a hornets' nest there a few months earlier, but the second was a sleepy place on the stagecoach route called Freeman's Pass. They spurred their horses hard as they caught the aroma of humanity drifting through the trees before them.

The ashen-faced Todd Fern rode in first as was his ritual and aimed his horse at the small well-used saloon that was placed carefully next to the Wells Fargo stage depot. The three riders followed slowly, never taking their eyes off the townspeople who watched them studiously.

Tubbs rode well for a fat man and drew level with Fern halfway down the long dry street. His features never seemed to change much when he was riding. He had learned to watch and be ready for the brave young fools who waved their weapons too freely in their direction.

Leeming and Evans rode behind their companions, as always taking in the things that Fern and Tubbs missed. The ride down the street was a long dry one which seemed to make all four riders nervous when they reached the pair of hitching rails before the noisy saloon.

Tubbs dismounted first and tied all four horses to the long poles whilst the three others satisfied themselves with the situation.

Then, and only then, did the other riders dismount and join their obese friend on the creaking sidewalk. They entered as one and moved through the crowd to the bar. Fern glanced at the clock which hung over the large mirror behind the two bartenders and screwed up his eyes.

The clock gave the time as being just after eleven in the morning.

'Is that the right time, buddy?' Fern asked the busy bartender closest to his men.

'It's right enough, stranger,' came the snappy reply.

'What's wrong, Todd?' Tubbs asked, rubbing his guts, feeling the pangs of hunger starting once again.

'I just never seen a saloon so busy this early before,' Fern replied, plucking out a handful of silver dollars and stacking them on the bar counter.

'Something must be up,' Leeming said striking a match along his chaps and putting the flame to his cigarette.

'You could be right,' Fern nodded as

the bartender came back for their orders.

'What'll it be?'

'Whiskey,' Fern answered. 'Four bottles.'

The man lifted up the stack of coins and quickly checked them before reaching under the bar and producing four bottles without labels. 'This good enough?'

Fern pulled a cork with his teeth and spat it down into a spittoon before tasting the liquor. 'Good enough.'

The four men drank from their bottles as they considered the activity within the long dark saloon. The bar girls were out in force plying their trade to the dozens of male customers within the long dark saloon. To see bar girls this early in the day was a strange sight in itself.

'I ain't seen a town so active before,' Tubbs noted.

'Not before noon, anyways,' Leeming added.

'You reckon they got females in this

joint?' Sonny Evans asked his friends as he swallowed his whiskey. 'I could sure use some company for an hour.'

Fern pointed at the far corner where the handful of girls were holding court amongst two dozen men. 'Can't you see them girls down in the corner Sonny?'

Evans stood to his full height and then noticed the women in their low-cut dresses and plumed headbands. A sudden awareness seemed to fill the killer's strange face as he started toward the gathering.

Tubbs shook his head. 'That boy is just plain pitiful.'

'Sad.' Leeming nodded in agreement with his rotund friend. 'Sonny don't think of nothing else. It's just plain sad.'

'I should be so sad,' Fern said lifting his bottle to his mouth again.

It was only a matter of seconds after Sonny Evans had forced his way into the heart of where the females were when all hell broke loose.

Fists started flying and men started crashing around in all directions. Evans was lifted by his belt and tossed across the saloon before crashing through a keno table. It was obvious to Fern that their young hothead had said, done or touched something that he shouldn't have.

The three men ran at the crowd of cowboys and started to try and fight their way through to the dazed Evans. It was not easy when the odds were four to one.

Tubbs took a punch on the chin and fell heavily onto his wide rear as an empty bottle came crashing over his skull. The splintering glass covered his worn Stetson as he fell onto his back and stared at the ceiling and the stars that he knew could not really be there although he could see them swirling around in his foggy vision.

Jeff Leeming smashed his fists into two men before him and managed to deck both before a chair found his back and sent him down. He lay with his mouth full of stale sawdust as Fern stepped over him and knocked a tall man over the bar onto the bartender.

Leeming felt a hand on his collar dragging him to his feet and, when he had regained his balance, he saw it was the still smiling Sonny Evans.

The two stepped into the crowd of men throwing punches as the half-dozen characters returned the knuckles. Leeming took one, two then three punches to his jaw before finding the man's chin with his solid uppercut. Teeth seemed to rain over the scene as Leeming followed the smaller Evans forward. A beer glass passed Fern's ear as he was pushed up against a wall by two men. Both his arms were pinned back as a third man delivered two crippling blows to his trim stomach. Fern felt his lungs empty of air as a third caught him under his ribs. Then he slid into the sawdust, gasping.

Tubbs felt a boot in his side. The kick seemed to clear his head and instinctively he grabbed the leg and twisted it in his strong large hands. The snapping noise echoed off the saloon walls as he tossed the man aside and rose to his feet. Tubbs could see a man with a knife getting ready to gut Todd Fern as he lay against the wall coughing. Charging at the man he crashed through everyone in his path until he hit the man off his feet and sent him bouncing into the stairs where the saloon girls had fled. The sound of the man's head breaking as it met the solid, wooden steps chilled even the large Tubbs who was dragging Fern to his feet.

Evans flew past them both as he crashed into the bar again with blood pouring from his mouth.

'You OK?' Tubbs asked the man.

Evans spat out a mouthful of blood and then smiled once more at his rotund friend. 'Sure am.'

Leeming was holding onto two men and trying in vain to wrestle them down into the sawdust. 'Help,' he yelled at his companions who all came racing to his assistance.

Tubbs kicked the man under Leeming's left arm in the head sending him immediately into another world. A world of dreams and nightmares.

Evans threw a short, solid right punch into the bridge of the other man's nose. Blood squirted everywhere as the force of the blow found its target. Leeming dropped both the men and got to his shaking feet as Fern caught hold of the legs of a chair that was about to be brought down on Leeming's skull. The tall gunfighter forced the man backward as they both stumbled and fell through a window out into the street. One last punch from Fern and the man lost his fight. Staggering through the glass Todd Fern scrambled back into the saloon to help his three men.

He fell onto one knee and then gasped in relief as he saw that only Tubbs, Leeming and Evans remained standing at the bar.

'Where ya been?' Tubbs asked, as he poured whiskey over his bleeding knuckles.

Fern got back up to his full height

and ambled across the floor littered with beaten men and blood. Lots of blood. Some of it his own.

'You go out for some air?' Leeming asked, as he nursed his bruised jaw.

'Yep.' Fern spat at the floor as he reached his bottle and took a mouthful of the rotgut. 'I thought I'd check the horses.'

Sonny Evans swilled his bleeding teeth with liquor and swallowed before heading for the girls on the stairs once more.

He was still smiling as he ascended the stairs with two of the prettiest.

Fern looked at Tubbs and then at Leeming. 'That kid will be the death of us one day, boys,' he muttered.

9

The small farmhouse lay in the middle of prime pastureland that was edged with trees of every variety. The grass was knee high and fit for the best cattle, the sort that grazed Hart Farm.

Trask stood on the porch watching the chickens pecking continuously at the ground before the farmhouse as he thought about the delicate female who had gone straight to her bed when they had arrived earlier. His features strained at the sight before him. It was so perfect that it beggared belief to this hard man. He struck a match and lit his cigarette before inhaling the blue smoke deeply.

As the smoke drifted back from his mouth his thoughts raced from one event to another. It was hard to figure what was occurring in this sweet valley but something was definitely not as it ought to be. This was a place where peace had ruled since time began and yet now evil had raised its ugly head and scarred the landscape forever.

Trask knew that only the greed of men brought such sorrow to communities such as this. The problem was he felt utterly helpless and unable to help. He had never stuck his nose into other folks' affairs before, but then, he had never seen such events so close up before either.

It was as if he felt compelled by a duty to Juliette Hart's dead father and the other ranchers who had been killed before his arrival. He had to try and help. Somehow he had to work out how he could achieve this goal. Trask was no lawman. He had skimmed the law for the past twenty years and somehow managed to stay on its right side. He was just one man yet this was a job for a small army.

Trask knew in his guts that the debonair Giles Davis was behind the trouble in the valley. He could taste it. Yet knowing something and proving it were two very different matters. It gnawed at him every time he pictured the face of Davis. He had never seen such a smug man as Davis although Trask admired his nerve. It took real nerve to face a man and lie through your teeth without breaking out in a sweat. Davis had nerve all right but whether the man had any morals was doubtful. Trask could not help but worry.

These people who lived and worked in the valley required help to cope with someone like Davis. How could Trask protect so many folks when he had no idea where or when the next fatal blow would be dealt? So many people living in so many remote farmhouses. He inhaled deeply again and watched as the sun dipped lower in the sky. Night was quickly approaching and darkness was when danger was at its most active.

Trask took hold of the glass bowl of the porch light and raised it before striking another match and lighting its wick. He lowered the glass and bathed in the orange glow of the light as it cast its illumination around the porch of the Hart farmhouse.

Finishing the cigarette he dropped it onto the flowerbed and watched as the evening dew ceased its burning.

This was a lovely farm, small and yet capable of sustaining itself. It had everything. Milk cows, beef cattle, poultry hens and egg producing chickens. Crops flourished in a fenced section beyond the grazing areas and a well pumped water in abundance into waiting barrels and troughs. The Hart farm might be small but it was self sufficient and Trask admired that.

Darkness was only a matter of minutes away and the gunfighter started to feel the chill of evening touching his bones as he lifted his gun-belt from the porch fence where it had been hanging since he put his horse in the barn earlier. He entered the house and closed the door behind him. He rested his gun-belt on a small table next to his Winchester and saddle-bags before proceeding to light every lamp in the main room.

Trask looked at the kitchen that adjoined the room and wondered what to do. He had not been in a real kitchen for over two decades and wondered how to prepare a meal. He had little idea of such things. On the trail he survived on jerky and when he entered towns or cities he allowed experts to cook his meals. This was something new for the man and after twenty minutes of failing to work it out he rested in a chair. Sleep came easily to the weary man, and when he awoke his nostrils told him something was happening.

Opening his eyes he saw Juliette Hart moving quietly around the kitchen busily and expertly. This was her domain and she ruled it like a queen. The aroma that had reached into his deep slumber and teased him until he awoke was wondrous. Trask had not enjoyed the smell of real cooking for many a year and it brought memories flooding back into his tired brain of long ago when he was younger than her. Years before she was born.

'So you finally woke up, Trask,' her voice said softly in an almost mocking tone.

'I have, ma'am,' he said rubbing the sleep from his eyes.

'It's ready.' She pointed to the table and the two chairs. She had set it for the meal. Two plates. Two cups in their saucers and cutlery.

Trask got to his feet and moved to the table. He felt rather embarrassed as he stood watching her work. 'You should be resting according to old Doc Vale.'

'Then we would both starve,' she said bluntly. 'Sit down.'

Trask complied with her orders and felt uneasy as she produced not only a fully cooked meal but coffee. 'This sure looks mighty fine, ma'am.'

'My name is Juliette,' she said placing the plate before him. 'As you saved my life, you may call me Juliette.'

'Gosh, this looks wonderful.' He drooled.

She sat down opposite him and stared at him. 'Trask?' she said calmly.

'Yes?' he found himself answering.

'I think you are a good man. A brave man,' she began, 'but when it comes to finding your way around a kitchen you are definitely a lost cause.'

Trask nodded in agreement. He felt his face start to get warm and knew that he was blushing. It had been a long time since he had blushed and was quite surprised that he was still capable of it.

'So you are here to look after me?' She toyed with her food with her fork.

'Yes.' He loosened his bandanna with his index finger.

'Should I pay you?'

'Do you need a hired hand around here?'

She thought about her father. 'I think that I do require someone to help with the chores.'

'Then I'll work for you.'

'I do not have much money, Trask,' she admitted.

'I'll work for food.' He smiled. 'I don't want your money.'

Juliette Hart looked hard at his features. She did not see a man who had lived almost as long as her late father, she saw a quiet-spoken man who had a few white hairs sprinkled around his face. She did not see wrinkles, she saw laughter lines that gave his face a certain charm and character.

Suddenly the room seemed brighter as both smiled across their plates at one another.

★ ★ ★

Coffeeville was unlike most towns when darkness paid its daily visit. Apart from the saloon, everything seemed to simply close and go to sleep. It was if the buildings themselves slept when the sun set and the stars came out. A few men with little to stay at home for would take a few drinks in the company of the

103

elderly bartender known as gramps. Everyone else just went to their neat homes and enjoyed the peaceful pleasures that most places had long forgotten.

The moon was still climbing its way in the sky when the four riders entered the township from the north. They rode slowly and as if pursued. The horses were steered to the hitching rails outside the saloon and the men dismounted. Todd Fern stepped up onto the sidewalk first and raised his hands to his three companions.

'No trouble,' Fern snarled at the men. 'We gotta get directions and then we leave for Davis's spread. OK?'

The men nodded.

The bartender was alone in the saloon except for Matt Hume, the butcher, who was sitting with a jug of beer before him. Both men looked up at the strange disturbing sight of the four men as they pushed their way into the saloon. Hume was a powerfully built man, as most men of his trade, yet even he did not feel safe as he watched the strangers making their way up to the bar.

'Four beers,' Fern said tossing a silver dollar onto the counter.

'Four beers it is.' The old man quickly filled four glasses with the amber liquid and placed them before the men.

Fern glared at his men in order that they stay under control and did not start anything. 'You happen to know where Giles Davis's place is, old-timer?'

'He's got an office a couple of doors down the way,' the old man replied.

'Not his office,' Fern said, after wiping the suds off his whiskered lips, 'we are looking for his spread.'

The bartender gave a little chortle as if amused by his own mistake and leaned on the bartop. 'You want his ranch. That's just down the trail.'

Fern and his men listened as they drank their beers and the old man gave them detailed directions. Somehow the four men managed to remain under

Fern's control during the conversation.

Matt Hume rose to his feet as the men walked from the saloon and mounted their animals outside. He leaned on the bar next to the old-timer as the men rode off into the darkness.

'You ever seen them around here before, gramps?' Hume asked, placing his empty jug next to the bartender to be refilled.

'Strangers, Matt.' The elderly man sniffed as he put the jug under the dripping beer tap. 'They are strangers, I reckon.'

Matt Hume watched as the beer started to flow into his jug and placed a dollar onto the bar. 'Very enlightening,' he frowned.

10

It was midnight when the sound of the four riders drew the attention of the assayer as he rested in a high-back chair reading one of his books. Giles Davis moved to one of the tall windows and stared down at the men as they pulled up beneath the window and began dismounting.

Davis marched out of the lavish room, across the dark hall before unlocking the large door and stepping out onto the lamp-lit porch. The sight that met his eyes pleased him. The four men were trail weary from their long ride that had taken far longer than any of them had expected when they started out. It was cold calculating eyes that stared up at the immaculate Davis upon the pristine porch. Davis watched silently as the men tied their mounts and dusted themselves off before turning in his direction.

It was Todd Fern who led the way up the steps, his three followers trailing in his long shadow. The tall man stared coldly at the man as he drew close as if smiling might cost him.

'Long time, Fern,' Davis said, holding out his hand in greeting.

Shaking the outstretched hand, Fern nodded. 'You can't imagine the trouble we've had finding this damn place, Davis. If it weren't for the map you sent me last month, I'd never have made it.'

'It don't pay to live out in the open, boys,' Davis said, as the men gathered around him. The smell of the long ride was heavy on the nostrils of the neatly dressed man.

Davis ushered the men inside and took them into the large gun room he kept for special visitors, whom he did not wish near his expensive collection of books and china. He noted the faces of the men change as they studied the room and its walls filled with weaponry. Fern and the others stared around the walls at the dozens of rifles and handguns. It was a collection that made a lot of people envious. The four hired gunmen were no exceptions.

'You've got yourself enough hardware here to equip an army, Davis,' Fern said, as he landed himself in the largest and most comfortable of the half-dozen leather chairs. 'You like guns?'

'I like guns.' Davis waved the men towards the trolleyful of hard liquor. 'Help yourselves, boys.'

They did.

Davis watched as each of his guests took a bottle each and seated themselves about the wood-panelled den. Soon the room was filled with their aroma; a mixture of human and horse sweat that tested even the most hardy of men.

The tired eyes of the four men watched as Giles Davis pulled out his thick, well-padded wallet and withdrew five fifty-dollar bills and tossed them into Todd Fern's lap. 'That's half up front, Fern. OK?'

Fern handed a bill to each of his three companions and tucked two into his vest pocket. 'You always was a good man to do business with,' he grinned.

'There might be a bonus if things go exactly the way I've planned,' Davis said, sliding the wallet into his inside jacket pocket.

'We gonna get fed?' Tubbs asked, as he swigged at his bottle heartily.

Davis moved to a hanging pull cord and gave it two tugs to inform his cook to start work. 'The meals will be ready soon.'

'What's the job?' Fern asked, as he unscrewed the top of the expensive whiskey bottle. 'It better be worth all our time and trouble, Davis.'

'Killing is the job,' Davis said bluntly. 'That good enough for you boys?'

'That's nice and easy,' Sonny Evans grinned.

'How many?' Fern questioned.

'Quite a lot,' Davis shrugged.

'This gets better and better, boys,' Leeming laughed.

Davis opened a box of cigars and watched as the men swooped on his expensive Havanas. He placed one in his mouth and struck a match. He pulled in the thick smoke and then sat down behind his desk. Soon the room was filled with a blue cloud as all the men puffed frantically on their cigars. 'You boys ever heard of a man named Trask?'

Todd Fern lowered his bottle and his cigar. 'Did you say Trask, Davis?'

Davis could see recognition in the killer's face. 'So you have heard of him, Fern?'

'I sure have heard of him. In fact I once met the man.' Fern sounded concerned. 'Is he here?'

'He's in the valley at the moment.' Davis puffed on his cigar as the smoke finally obliterated the smell of the riders. 'I don't know why he's hanging around but he is.'

'Who is this Trask?' Evans asked innocently, staring around the faces of his companions.

'He's bad news, Sonny,' Tubbs replied. 'I heard that he is the very best gunfighter alive.'

'Real bad news for us,' Leeming added.

Todd Fern sat on the edge of his chair staring through the trailing cigar smoke. 'They say Trask ain't human. They say he's some kinda magician and his guns are bewitched.'

'Hogwash.' Tubbs roared with laughter until he felt the hand of Jeff Leeming on his shoulder. Then he knew he should quit laughing. Tubbs stopped laughing.

'You serious?' Evans asked the grey-faced man who seemed in a trance as he stared into the rising smoke from his Havana.

'Yep,' Fern replied softly.

'You scared of this Trask critter, Fern?' Giles Davis stared hard at the man who had gone rather quiet.

Fern narrowed his eyes and glanced at the assayer. 'I seen him in a showdown once, Davis. I never seen anyone as fast or as accurate as Trask was that day.'

'You say his guns are magic?' Sonny Evans flicked the ash off his cigar onto the polished boards.

Fern's face was like a death mask as he visualized the scene long ago when he had witnessed the man known as Trask in that showdown. 'I never seen anything like that before or since, Sonny. It was like his guns had a mind of their own.'

'Is he as fast as they say?' Giles Davis suddenly felt the trepidation which emanated from the hired gunfighter.

'He is.' Fern took a shot of his whiskey. 'He sure is.'

11

Coffeeville remained quiet for the whole of the following day but once the sun had set again, trouble seemed to drift on the air like a bad smell.

Big Joe Cooper closed the giant doors of his livery and stood in the shadows searching in his leather apron for the key that would secure the massive lock. Normally he never locked the door, but as the sunlight disappeared and darkness came, he felt a strange feeling overwhelm him: it was fear.

He stood in the dark where the street lamp's illumination could not penetrate and turned the key. He had lived in Coffeeville his entire thirty-two years and yet this was the first time that he had sensed any danger. It was a new emotion that he did not like nor understand.

Then he heard the sound of horses. Without even knowing why, he stepped back into the bushes near his small house and waited for the riders to pass him. Thirty seconds later, they did.

Cooper's eyes screwed up as he focused upon the familiar figure of Giles Davis leading the group of rough riders past the livery and on towards the assayer's office. Five men, four of whom were totally unknown to Cooper. He stood unable to move for a few seconds before heading slowly across the dark street and up onto the boardwalk. Cautiously, the stableman headed down towards the men as they dismounted outside Davis's office.

For a big man, Cooper somehow managed to walk quietly enough so the five men did not notice his approach. Pausing for a moment, Cooper watched as they all entered the dark office. A moment later the golden glow spread out from the window of the office into the street as a lamp was lit. As Cooper started to walk towards the light he saw the light disappear as the shade was pulled down.

Joe Cooper continued slowly until he was standing next to the office window. He leaned into the window pressing his ear against the glass as his eyes watched the five mounts tied up before the sidewalk.

He strained hard to listen to what was being said for a moment when he heard a voice calling to him from down the street. Turning quickly he saw the baker Bert Hartnell heading toward the saloon.

'Joe?' Hartnell shouted again.

Cooper moved away from the window and quickly walked toward the man who was covered in flour. 'Bert,' he said to the baker, his thoughts remaining on the men inside the small office.

'Coming in for a drink?' Hartnell asked, as he rested a hand on the swing doors of the saloon.

Cooper stood open-mouthed for a second. Then he heard the door of the assayer's office open behind him and the sound of feet on the boardwalk. Sweat ran down his broad back as he knew someone was staring at him hard and long. 'Sure, Bert. I was looking for you. Let's drink us some beer.'

Cooper moved into the bright saloon with the baker and headed for the bar and the elderly bartender. His heart was pounding inside his shirt like a hammer hitting an anvil. Joe Cooper had never been so terrified in all his life. Staring at the mirror behind the bar he caught a brief glimpse of Giles Davis. Davis then returned to his office.

'What's eating you, Joe?' Hartnell asked, as they rested their arms on the wooden bar top.

Cooper could not speak. He just leaned on the counter waiting for his heart to stop beating the hell out of his ribs.

★ ★ ★

The darkness now ruled where daylight had reigned until the sun dipped below the distant mountain which towered above the valley. For nearly an hour since the sun had set and the cold black of night overwhelmed the farm, Trask had stood alone on the porch rolling, then smoking, cigarettes. The aroma of supper cooking drifted from the farmhouse as he took in the scenery. He had worked hard for the female known as Juliette Hart and tried to do everything he thought her late father would have done. Taking the place of a dead man made Trask uneasy, but he knew that he had to stay close to the woman. There was a feeling in his bones that her life might be the next to be taken by whoever had killed Thomas Hart. Since saving her life when she was on the runaway buckboard he felt somehow responsible for her. Striking another match, Trask lit the porch lamp and gazed out at the scene before him.

Then he saw something out on the distant horizon that drew his attention.

It was a rider cutting through the trees and heading straight towards him. Trask watched with an intensity that had served him well over the years.

The last thing Trask had expected to see as he stood taking in the early evening air on the porch of the Hart farmhouse was Joe Cooper riding towards him. Yet that was what Trask saw as he sucked on his cigarette. Trask knew something had to be very wrong for such a large man to get onto a horse and ride so far in the darkness. Clouds filled the sky and few stars could be seen as the moon drifted in and out of view. With only the light of the full moon to guide him, Cooper had ridden from Coffeeville for a pretty important reason, Trask concluded.

The rider aimed his horse at the lamp on the wall behind Trask and reached the house safely. Trask stepped down from the porch and grabbed the reins from Cooper who slowly dismounted.

'Trouble, Joe?' Trask asked quietly, as

he secured the reins to the hitching rail.

Cooper nodded, trying to get his wind back. It had been years since he had ridden a horse and it showed. 'Yeah. Trouble.'

'Explain.' Trask sat down on the steps of the porch and watched as the big man rested a foot next to him. 'What has got you so fired up that you had to ride out here at this hour?'

Cooper looked down at Trask. 'I might be just letting my imagination run away with me . . . '

'I reckon you ain't the sort to have much of an imagination, Joe.' Trask stared hard through the moonlight at the man. 'Spit it out.'

'Davis came into town after sundown with four men.' Cooper took a deep breath.

'What kinda men?' The gunfighter felt the hairs on the nape of his neck starting to tingle as he listened carefully to the big man's words.

'Strangers,' Cooper said darkly. 'I ain't never seen them before and they looked mean. They look like hired guns.'

'So you ain't ever seen these men before.' Trask pulled out his tobacco pouch and started to roll another smoke as he thought about the situation.

Cooper rested his bones next to the gunfighter. 'Davis must have brought these men in for a reason, Trask.'

'To replace Carver.' Trask licked the gummed paper and rolled the cigarette carefully in his fingers.

Cooper watched as the older man struck a match and drew it to the end of his cigarette. The smoke drifted out from between the teeth of the man who then offered it to the larger man. Cooper took a long pull on the thin smoke before returning it to Trask's waiting fingers. 'Was I right to come and tell you?'

'Yep, Joe,' Trask nodded, as he inhaled once more. 'I reckon you did the right thing.'

The door of the farmhouse opened

behind the two men and bathed them in the warm light of the numerous lamps. The smell of cooking filled the air as the men rose to their feet and stepped up onto the porch.

'Hello, Joe.' Juliette Hart greeted the big man with surprise written across her face. 'I had no idea you were here.'

'Joe just rode in, Juliette,' Trask said, moving past her into the warmth of the house.

She watched passively as Trask picked up his gun-belt from the small table beside the front window of the house. 'What's wrong, Trask?'

Trask checked his weapons before returning them to their holsters and slipping the safety loops over the hammers. His face gazed at her briefly as he plucked his Stetson off the hook next to the door and placed it onto his head. 'Nothing's wrong.'

Trask walked out between the two people he had grown to like, and then paused above the steps. Turning slowly he looked at them both. 'I'm heading into town to check something out.'

Cooper moved towards the man and was surprised when Trask raised a hand to stop him.

'Stay here with Juliette, Joe,' Trask said firmly. 'My Winchester is beside the armchair if you need it.'

'But — ?' Cooper started to speak but his words were cut short by the man before him.

'Mind if I borrow your horse?'

Cooper shrugged. 'You can borrow my horse but why do I have to stay here?'

'Just in case visitors pay a call.' Trask walked down to the horse and ran his hand along the creature's neck whilst hanging the buckled belt over the saddle horn. 'Get my drift, Joe?'

'Yep. I gets your drift, Trask.' Cooper tucked his thumbs into his belt and watched as Trask mounted the horse before pulling the reins free of the hitching rail.

'Trask?' Juliette Hart's voice seemed to beckon answers from the gunfighter.

Answers that were not forthcoming.

'Joe will stay here until I return, Juliette,' Trask said as he turned the horse away from the rail. 'Maybe you can give him a spot of supper.'

The two watched as Trask rode the horse hard down into the blackness. The howls of a distant coyote drifted across the courtyard as they stood silently in his wake. Trask was heading to Coffeeville. He had no idea why but every bone in his body knew that it was the thing to do.

Davis was trouble; Trask knew it. Now he had four men to back him up. The only thing that eluded Trask as he stood in the stirrups and galloped towards the distant town, was why. Why would a man like Giles Davis surround himself with hired guns? Why would a man who was just a simple assayer be able to live in such a lavish manner?

Trask gritted his teeth and rode hard down the trail through the dense trees and past the lush moonlit pastures. Every long stride of Cooper's horse brought him closer to Coffeeville. Closer to the chance of gaining answers to the questions that burned into his soul.

* * *

The five riders who stayed hidden in the thick bushes and tall broad-leafed trees, waited. Giles Davis had never before done his own dirty work, but the thought of being there when the famous Trask finally met his Maker was too tempting for the sly man. He had led the four hired killers from his place to this remote farm avoiding the main trail that wound its way along the floor of the valley. They had travelled slowly through the thick woodland that edged most of the farms, arriving at their vantage point overlooking the Hart place just as the rider galloped past them in the darkness.

'Who was that, Davis?' Todd Fern asked the assayer as they carefully controlled their horses in the bushes.

The heavy cloud cover nearly obliterated the full moon for several minutes after their arrival at the edge of the Hart spread and Davis could see as little as his men. He had recognized the saddle though.

'Who was that?' Sonny Evans repeated Fern's question.

'I think it was the livery-stable owner,' Davis said rubbing his chin. 'He has a real fancy saddle like that.'

'What was he doing out here?' Leeming asked quietly, watching the distant farmhouse with its warm glow drifting through the open doorway.

'Joe Cooper is a pal of Trask's,' Davis assumed. 'I figure he was just out here keeping the man informed.'

Fern pulled his horse out onto the trail and looked down the dark avenue of trees. 'Well, he's gone now.'

Davis was nervous as he sat in his saddle amid the ruthless men he had hired. Yet for all his nerves an excitement kept his heart beating at an incredible rate. He had never before been involved in a raid. The sheer thought of it was making him feel ten years younger. 'We had better wait for ten minutes, boys.'

'Why wait?' Tubbs asked angrily.

'Yeah, why should we wait?' Evans butted in.

Davis raised himself in his saddle and smelt the air. 'Can you smell that?'

The four men sniffed the air.

'I can smell food cooking,' Tubbs said, saliva running from the corners of his mouth.

'Exactly,' Davis said, gripping the saddle horn before him tightly. 'We let Trask and the girl sit down and eat their supper and then we attack.'

'Food makes a soul slow and sleepy.' Fern grinned in the light of the moon that was just starting to fight its way free of the clouds above their heads.

'And the longer we wait, the closer Cooper gets to Coffeeville and further away from here.' Davis was starting to think like the vermin he employed. 'We don't want Cooper turning back and helping Trask, do we?'

Sonny Evans pulled his horse closer to the elegant man and smiled his usual sickly smile. 'You say there's a girl down there in the farmhouse, Davis?'

'Sure. Juliette Hart. Why?' Giles Davis looked into the eyes of the man who was sitting smiling as he thought about the female inside the house.

'She pretty?' Evans asked coyly.

'What?' Davis did not understand the small man's line of questioning. Yet he recognized the smile and the look on Sonny Evans's face.

'You do what you're ordered to do, Sonny,' Fern snapped at the man who had a problem with females. He could never walk past one however ugly they were. 'You do as you're ordered. OK?'

Sonny Evans gave a sick smile as he stared at the distant house. 'Sure, Fern. I'll do as you say.'

Somehow none of his four companions believed the words that ran like spit from Evans's mouth.

Ten minutes later the five men rode silently onto the trail and started to make their way towards the farmhouse. They spread out across the grassy pastures and started to circle the house until they had it completely surrounded. Then they put their plan into operation and pulled out the five oil-soaked torches they had prepared earlier at Davis's place. Each man lit his torch and stood for a few moments holding the flaming death sticks above their heads. Each man could see at least two of his companions as they sat on their mounts in a circle around the pristine farmhouse.

It was Davis who signalled the others to do their worst. The five men rode towards the house quickly and silently. When they were within feet of their target, they tossed the fiery torches through windows and under the raised baseboard foundation. Then they began to circle as the fire took hold. Screams and shouts came from the interior of the building as its occupants suddenly realized they were being burned out.

Davis's men kept their distance as they waited with their carbines drawn and ready. The house must have been tinder dry as the fire engulfed the structure far faster than any of them anticipated.

Suddenly Todd Fern yelled and pointed to the rear of the building as two souls came crashing out of the kitchen doorway into the courtyard.

All five riders rode hard after the two shadowy figures. Shots rang out from the flowerbed where the big man had placed himself between the approaching raiders and the distressed Juliette Hart.

Fern returned the fire far faster than Joe Cooper was able to use the Winchester. Fern watched as the big man dropped his weapon and staggered wounded around the building before cocking his rifle again and blasting the man in the back.

Cooper fell into the sweet-smelling flowers and tried to turn to face his attackers. Evans rode up to the man and blasted at the huge chest below him. He did not quit until he had used every bullet in his rifle.

Davis rode after Fern and looked down at the dead stableman and then went pale. 'This is Cooper.'

'I thought you said Cooper lit out?' Fern said, as he studied the body, the flames leaping out above their heads.

'That must have been Trask on Cooper's horse,' Davis gasped with a sense of urgency in his voice.

'Damn,' Fern snarled, as Tubbs and Leeming drew up beside them and pointed to what Sonny Evans was up to.

'Sonny caught himself a girl, Fern.' Tubbs pointed at the crazed Evans who was standing above the fallen female tearing at her clothes with one hand with his Colt in the other.

Davis went to ride at the young killer when Fern grabbed his reins.

'Stay out of it, Davis.' Fern advised.

'Why?' Davis asked, as Juliette Hart's screams echoed around the courtyard. The assayer could not believe his eyes as he watched the young man destroying her. The sight was more than any of the men could handle for long yet they had seen it before far too many times.

'Sonny is kinda crazy, Davis,' Todd Fern said quietly.

'Couldn't you stop him?'

'That would be rather dangerous.' Leeming said. 'When his steam is up it ain't safe to get close.'

Then they heard the shots that ended the screams from the young woman beneath Sonny Evans. All four men sat in their saddles until the laughing Evans had finished. They watched him getting back into his saddle before they rode towards him. Nothing was said as the five riders rode hard into the woodland and back towards the Davis spread. As they rode through the trees each of the men felt the cold shiver running up their spines as Sonny Evans continued

132

laughing to himself. Each rider knew Evans had taken a trophy to remind him of what he had done to the fragile Hart girl. They could see him toying with something in his hands as they continued riding. None of them had any desire to find out what it was.

The flames behind them began to reach heavenward, sending two souls to a more peaceful place.

12

Coffeeville was almost vacant of light as Trask galloped in. The miles had melted away beneath the hooves of Cooper's strong horse and he had made good time. He pulled the mount to a stop in the centre of the long tree-lined street. The street lamps glowed pitifully as Trask looked around the buildings for signs of life beside the saloon. There were no horses tied up anywhere in the town. The mature rider rode to the livery and then back down to the end of the one-street town. There was nothing to be seen anywhere. It was an eerie silence that dominated the small town and Trask began to wonder if his long ride had been wise. His thoughts found their way to the man called Davis. A man who had more than any man deserved to have and no real means of ever getting so much legally. Trask had faced dozens of men with guns in his day and that had never concerned him, but a man who hid behind a smile and a fancy suit was different. Such a man paid for his dirty work to be done. Such men never got their hands dirty and yet they were more dangerous than those they hired.

Trask rode toward the silent saloon and dismounted. He dropped the reins and walked into the well-illuminated drinking place and stopped as the swing doors flapped back and forth behind him.

Two men sat near the long bar where the familiar old man stood silently. Coffeeville was like a graveyard after dark and only the dedicated few seemed to be able to function without sunlight upon their spines. Trask glanced around and studied the place as if expecting the wallpaper to draw down upon him.

Ten paces brought Trask to the man

standing behind a stack of gleaming glasses. 'You seen Davis in here tonight?'

'Not tonight, Trask,' the man replied lifting up a beer glass and placing it under the tap. 'Beer on the house?'

Trask paused for a second. He was dry but not that dry. A sudden urgency filled his heart as he tried to work out what his next move ought to be. 'No thanks. I reckon I made a mistake in coming into town tonight.'

Trask felt as if the words he had just spoken were haunting him even as they left his dry lips. Suddenly he knew that this was not where he ought to be. He should still be back at the Hart Farm.

The bartender watched as a very troubled Trask marched out from the saloon into the dark street and gathered up his reins before placing his foot into the awaiting stirrup and pulling himself onto the horse. There seemed no way that Trask could hide the worry that etched itself across his face. Gently tapping his feet against the horse's sides, Trask walked the horse past the assayer's office and leaned down to take a good look at the window with the gold paint on it. Trask looked long and hard at the window before straightening up again. There was no sign of life in the small office.

Pulling up his reins the horse stopped and Trask stared down at the ground beside the hitching pole. The fertile earth was torn up and evidence that Joe Cooper had been correct. At least five mounts had been standing here earlier. Trask bit his lip and wondered what his next move should be and then decided that he would head back to the Hart Farm.

As he kicked the horse into flight, a cold shiver ran over his spine. As he galloped into the countryside he felt as if he had been lured here. The harder he rode the more desperate his feelings became.

The trail was eaten up fast under the hooves of his borrowed horse as he forced the creature on. The farm was far away and to get there quickly he had to drive this horse harder than anyone had ever done before. Trask leaned over the neck of the horse whispering encouragement into its ear as he stood high in the stirrups balancing like a carnival tightrope walker.

Trask rode like he had never ridden before in all his twenty years of roving. Twenty years of always heading forward and never looking or going back. A time when months evaporated into years. Lost years. Now he felt something that he had never felt before in all those years. A sense of urgency overwhelmed him and that scared him. Somehow he had allowed feelings to find their way through his armour and make him concerned for someone apart from himself. As Trask galloped on and on he knew that fear was gnawing at his guts. Not the fear of a man who is afraid for his own safety but the fear that something might be happening to others he had somehow become fond of.

The journey that ought to have taken a good half-hour was completed in only twenty minutes. Trask had no feelings of mercy for the horse beneath him, all he could think about was the man and woman at the distant farmhouse in the middle of nowhere.

As he hurtled along the tree-lined trail he saw the fire rising high into the dark sky off in the distance. As hard as he tried, he could not make the creature beneath him travel any faster.

The closer he got the more his nostrils were filled with the acrid smell of burning.

13

Trask had witnessed many things over the past forty plus years but nothing like the sight that rose before him as he rode toward the Hart farmhouse. The horse spooked as the flames licked around in the night breeze and Trask pulled up short. The heat that came from the blazing house burned Trask's face as he stepped off the lathered horse.

Standing next to the frightened animal, gripping the reins tightly, Trask stood open-mouthed, helplessly watching. There had never been such a blaze outside Hell itself in its totality and sheer viciousness. There was a pain inside him that he had never known before. A pain that comes from grief. Tying his reins to a sapling, Trask ventured towards the building nervously wondering what horrors awaited him, dreading what he knew he might find and fearing his own reaction. The heat kept him at a distance like an invisible wall that forced Trask to walk around the building slowly. Flames licked up into the sky sending black clouds that completely obliterated the full moon.

Then, as he found himself at the rear of the blazing house, Trask stopped and saw the large man lying on his back in what once had been a flower garden. Moving with his hand shielding his face from the searing temperature, Trask managed to grab hold of the collar of the man and used all his strength to drag the bulk away to a cooler safer place.

The choking smoke that swirled around him as he strained his every muscle pulling the heavy body to safe ground, burned his eyes and his lungs.

Trask fell onto his knees and looked at the face of Joe Cooper and knew the man was dead. In the light of the flames he could see the bullet holes in the man's shirt. Only one bullet hole had traces of blood and Trask knew the others had been fired into the body after Cooper had died. The brave big man had been used for target practice. The taste of bitterness filled Trask's mouth as he closed the man's vacant eyelids. Sadness poured over him momentarily. It was a sadness that Trask had not experienced before as he shook with emotion. Getting back onto his feet Trask began searching around the building again as flames roared upward and outward in the night breeze. Exploding wood sent showers of red burning splinters in all directions as Trask moved, yet he did not notice. There was only one thought filling the gunfighter's mind and that was the fear of finding his anxieties were well founded. His heart pounded frantically in his chest with every step he took. Then he stopped and felt his soul screaming at the sight ahead of him.

Half hidden in the long grass that edged the corral beside the untouched barn he saw her naked legs. Clenching his fists, he managed to force himself to walk towards the legs. Part of him prayed that she were still alive. That she were just stunned and easily fixed up. When his eyes finally were able to focus onto all of her, he knew that death had saved her from further torture. Only God could fix her wounds, he thought.

Even the coyotes in the distant hills could not compete with the agonizing scream that came from Trask as he cradled the lifeless body of Juliette Hart in his strong arms.

14

Giles Davis stood beside his roaring fire tossing logs into its white-hot heart. He was not his normal debonair self and had not noticed the black, charcoal stains that covered his fine clothing. This night had been like no other for the dishonest assayer. This night he had not just sent his hired killers to do his bidding, he had participated. The four hired men had all gone to their beds upstairs in his massive home. Davis gloated in the fact that his men had achieved what they had been paid to achieve. He was one step closer to his ultimate goal. The fire roared but not nearly as brightly as the Hart farmhouse had burned earlier. Only one thing had soured the evening's event: Trask had not been at the farm.

Davis paced around the large room smoking his long cigars and drinking his expensive liquor. He knew that he ought to be content but he was not. Trask was the joker in the pack and he was out there someplace.

He had four ruthless gunmen in his employ and yet he was beginning to experience fear. Davis knew he ought to have nothing to fear from anyone in the valley but then he thought of the mysterious Trask. The unfathomable Trask and the guns that he had yet to strap around his middle like any ordinary man. Davis was sweating as he poured himself another brandy.

It was the sweat that only comes from the pores of a man who knows his days are numbered.

To look at Trask was an old man compared to himself but that did not stop Davis from sweating. For the first time since he had started his evil plan, Davis felt as if he had made a mistake. A very big mistake. Trask was no man to have as an enemy by all the stories that had been told of him over the years. Attacking the Hart place seemed like a good idea when he and his four men had set out earlier. For some reason Trask was not in the farmhouse with the Hart girl. He had not been there for his killers to gun down. Why hadn't Trask been there protecting Juliette Hart? Why was Cooper there? None of it made any sense and the more he drank the less sense it made.

Giles Davis finished his drink and poured himself another as he brooded over the error. The brandy bottle had been sealed when he had arrived back with his men, now there was a mere four fingers remaining in the bottle.

Killing Trask with the Hart girl would have allowed him to complete his plan quickly with little or no resistance, but Trask had not been there. Davis moved towards the large window and stumbled into a massive vase sending it crashing to the polished wood floor and splintering into a hundred fragments.

The sight of the valuable vase broken at his feet would normally have sent the assayer into a frenzy, yet that was before the deeds he had participated in. Now all he could think about was Trask. He knew Trask would find the bodies and then come after him. Sweat dripped from his face into the crystal tumbler as he stared at the brown liquor.

Swinging around as he heard footsteps behind him, Davis glared at the figure of Todd Fern standing in the doorway. Fern had been awoken by the sound of the breaking vase and decided to investigate. Standing in his worn red long-johns with his gun gripped firmly in his hand, he looked a rather pathetic figure.

'Fern,' Davis gulped. 'I thought you were . . . '

'What the hell is eating at you, Davis?' Fern asked, rubbing his eyes and yawning. 'Smashing up your priceless trinkets at this hour?'

'I was thinking about Trask.' The expression that was carved across the face of Davis drew Fern closer.

Fern rubbed his neck. 'Maybe he lit

out before we got to that farm. He is a drifter.'

'Nope. He's still in the valley somewhere.' Davis swallowed his brandy and leaned onto the back of an armchair. 'We made a real bad mistake killing them folks.'

'That could make things a mite dangerous.' Fern walked to the side of the man who still had the black smoke marks on his face and clothes.

'Do you think he'll come after us?' Davis's eyes were begging for an answer that he knew would not be given.

'Trask is a strange one,' Fern said, pouring himself a drink and then sipping it. 'Mighty strange they say.'

'Strange?' Davis wiped his face on his sleeve and noticed the grime that was embedded into the expensive material.

'Yep. He's the sort to fight other folk's battles for them,' Fern said. 'I call that pretty damn strange.'

Davis knew there was another word for such actions. For such men. Men who championed others weaker than themselves. Men who fought on the side of justice with never a thought for recompense. The word wasn't strange, thought Giles Davis; the word was gallant.

15

The sight that befell the eyes of the residents of Coffeeville an hour after sunrise made each and every one of them stop what they were doing and be drawn like moths to a naked flame. Within a matter of seconds it seemed that every resident of the small town was out on the sidewalks watching the approaching vehicle as it carefully manoeuvred towards them.

Trask sat on the high driving seat of the buckboard grim faced as he slowly drove the matched two-horse team up the trail towards the small township. Behind the buckboard, two horses were tied to the raised tailgate, Joe Cooper's horse on the left and his own chestnut, Smoke, on the right. As Trask made his way towards Doc Vale's place he constantly looked over his broad shoulder onto the flatbed behind him as if waiting for a miracle to occur and the two lifeless bodies to be miraculously restored.

The faces of men and women as they watched the solemn sight were pale and concerned. They all recognized the Hart buckboard and they all knew Trask, but this did not seem right to any of them. They had all seen Trask's face before when he had brought in the body of Tom Hart. His expression was exactly the same now as he steered the team along the street. Trask had pain written in every weathered line upon his face.

Pulling on the long leather reins, he pushed his foot down hard on the brake pole and waited for the vehicle to stop. It seemed as if every living soul in Coffeeville had gathered around the buckboard as it stopped outside the white picket fence of the doctor's home. Trask wrapped the reins tightly around the brake pole rising and stepping carefully onto the flatbed. Kneeling down he drew back the large

151

weatherproof tarp revealing the two bodies. Men as well as women gasped at the horrific sight and yet Trask saw nor heard any of them.

Only Trask knew the body of the fragile female he had known so briefly had been stripped clean of all her clothes either before or after she had been murdered. It was clear to him that she had been abused either before or after she was killed. Trask had dressed her as best he could with the torn fragments of clothing he had been able to find around the burned-out farmhouse.

Stooping, he gently scooped up her limp body in his arms and carried it to the back of the buckboard. Two men lowered the tailgate and supported him as he carefully found the ground with his high-heeled boots. All assistance was rejected as he carried Juliette Hart to the waiting doctor who escorted him inside his home.

Only the doctor and the gunfighter knew what was said within the confines of those four square walls but the horrified crowd had a pretty good idea. Death had come back to the sweet valley and claimed two more victims.

On leaving the house, Trask's eyes caught sight of the undertaker and several men carrying the heavy body of Joe Cooper away towards his parlour. Trask screwed up his eyes as he headed through the crowd.

His face was grim as he carried on walking back to his waiting horse. He looked like a man devoid of any remaining emotions except one. Only revenge seemed to lurk behind the tanned lined face of Trask. Men and women buzzed around him as if he were wounded himself. He seemed unable to hear anything any of them were saying to him. He heard the sounds but the words were meaningless. His mind was numb with pain. His only thought was to untie Smoke from the back of the buckboard and get those who had destroyed two gentle people.

Then the strong hand of Matt Hume gripped Trask by the upper arm and somehow managed to make contact with the gunfighter. Trask stared into the face of the butcher and nodded. It was clear to anyone with eyes to see that Trask was hurting very badly. Somehow after all the years of self-indulgence, he had finally been hurt. Not by the bullets of his many challengers but by emotion itself. Trask had allowed a woman to enter his soul but she was gone like the brief scent of a wild rose.

'You OK, Trask?' Hume asked, staring into the face of the gunfighter.

'Nope,' Trask replied trying to avoid eye contact with anyone. 'I ain't ever been less OK.'

'What happened here, man?'

'Murder.' Trask pulled his reins free of the tailgate. 'Cold-blooded murder.'

'Who did it?' The butcher seemed genuinely concerned and that meant a lot to the gunfighter.

'I've got a good idea.' Trask stepped

into his stirrup and pulled himself into his saddle and patted the gun-belt that hung over the saddle horn. 'I've a damn good idea.'

'You want our help, man?' Hume looked like a man who could pull the head off a mustang if he had a mind.

'This ain't a job for nice folks,' Trask replied, as he turned Smoke's head to face the direction from where he had just arrived.

'Wait up and I'll get us at least a dozen men to ride with you.' Hume seemed confident that he could do as he promised.

For a moment Trask was tempted by the thought of having men with him, but then knew he was always at his best when he was alone. 'You just take care of Joe.'

'Wait man,' Hume said again. 'Let us help you catch these bastards.'

Trask looked at the faces of the people who were all standing around his horse. Faces that were good, honest, hard-working ones. These were the sort of people he had been searching for all his days. It seemed he had found his paradise either too early or too late.

'You folks are kinda special,' Trask said, looking down at his gun-belt wrapped around the saddle horn before him. 'What I gotta do ain't the kinda thing good folks should ever do. Your hands are clean and free of the dirt that haunts the hands of ruthless killers. You don't want blood on your hands because it don't ever wash off. Believe me. No matter how hard you scrub it never washes off.'

Matt Hume patted the neck of Trask's mount as he spoke. 'You are a mighty brave man, Trask. Fighting other men's battles for them. Fighting our enemies.'

'I ain't brave,' Trask corrected the butcher, 'I'm just angry. And you're wrong, this is my fight. Somebody made it real personal last night. Now they are gonna pay.'

'You take care, Mr Trask,' a frail female voice said to his right.

Trask sought out the voice and saw an elderly woman who was buckled by the passage of time. He returned her smile. 'I'll try, ma'am, I'll surely try.'

The gunfighter turned his chestnut stallion and aimed its nose at the open trail. Trask slapped his reins and drove his reliable horse hard down the street past the neat rows of buildings. Soon clouds of dust rose into the morning air. The crowd watched with a mixture of admiration and pride as the rider galloped away in the direction of Giles Davis's place. There were some who wondered if the man would win his fight and find the justice he sought.

16

The strong chestnut galloped onto the grounds of the Davis spread and straight up to the huge front door. Without waiting for Smoke to stop, Trask leapt to the ground clutching both his weapons in his strong hands. The horse came to a stop at his side and waited for its master to do whatever it was he was about to do. Trask marched up the steps and kicked the door in with a single strike from his left boot. A sprinkling of dust fell from the wooden joist as the doors crashed into the interior walls. Trask entered the house behind his outstretched guns. They were leading him as always and this was one time when he followed willingly.

Apart from a few servants the house was empty, he concluded, after searching each and every room. The utility rooms at the rear of the large building were the final ones he entered as he took the small, spiral, servants' staircase down from the bedrooms above.

Trask stopped as he encountered the terrified female servant who was sorting out bundles of laundry. He paced towards her silently and plucked the garments from the basket. He recognized the suit as being one of Giles Davis's. The black stains that covered it and its matching shirt made the gunfighter's eyes narrow. The small woman shook nervously as she watched Trask raise the clothes to his nose. The aroma of coal oil lingered powerfully as Trask turned away from her and dropped the clothes to the floor. He knew that the arsonists who had burned the Hart farmhouse had used torches wrapped in sackcloth and soaked in coal oil. He had found the remains of one such torch only eight feet from Juliette Hart's broken body.

'Who are you, mister?' the servant asked fearfully.

Trask turned towards her. His eyes were burning with tears as the sunlight drifted through the long window. 'My name ain't worth a damn, honey,' he said sorrowfully.

'Why you waving them guns around in Mr Davis's house?' She shook as she spoke.

'Where is he and the men he hired?' Trask asked, trying to stop the emotion revealing itself further.

'You gonna kill them?'

Trask could feel his heart pounding against his breast-bone as he moved past her. 'Maybe. All I want to know is where they are. Do you have any notion?'

The woman suddenly seemed to sense that this was no useless trash like the men she had noticed hanging around the house earlier. This man was grieving. 'They headed out to the Johnson farm, real early.'

'How long ago did they leave?' Trask felt the blood in his veins rushing through his body as the perception of what they were about to do hit him.

'Early. Maybe five-thirty.' She watched as he edged towards the door which led through the house to the elegant frontage.

'Which direction is the Johnson farm?'

'It's right up the trail at the foot of the mountain.'

Trask nodded and pushed the door ajar before pausing to look back at the woman whose hands were red and wrinkled. 'I'm sorry I scared you, ma'am. It wasn't my intention. I apologize.'

She watched as he ran through the building towards the busted front doors and into the daylight. She had lived for over fifty years and never before been spoken to in such a respectful manner.

Trask grabbed the reins of Smoke and slipped the guns into their holsters on the gun-belt hanging from the saddle horn before swinging himself up into his saddle. Kicking the stallion firmly he headed back out from the courtyard onto the valley trail. He knew exactly where the washer-woman had meant and remembered passing several farms a few days earlier having finally reached the fertile valley from the mountain trail.

Trask stood in his stirrups and urged the horse to gallop faster than it had ever done before. Whoever this Johnson character was, his life was in danger and Trask knew that he had stomached enough killing over the past twelve hours to last him a lifetime. If he was able, he would stop the carnage before the valley was swimming in the blood of innocents.

Smoke raced along the narrow trail like a horse half his years responding to the gentle encouragement his rider gave him. It was a long ride down the dusty makeshift road between massive proud trees and green lush fields filled with crops and livestock. The further he rode, the darker the trail became as the trees grew taller and broader in the shadow of the tall mountain.

The trail forked in two directions ahead of him and Trask knew both had to lead to the end of the valley. A decision had to be made quickly as the horse thundered on beneath him. If he chose the wrong route a life might be the price of his mistake. Gritting his teeth he dragged his reins to the left and allowed the horse to charge down the leafy glade that edged the sparkling, ice-cold stream. This was the narrower of the two trails but Trask had a gut feeling it was the shortest route to his destination. Now it seemed as if the branches above him were getting lower and far more dense but he continued his desperate pace.

Faster and faster he drove the horse on as the trail became narrower and narrower with trees and wild bushes on either side. The horse continued to gallop down the trail blindly obeying the urgency in his rider's hands as they gripped the reins tightly. Throwing caution to the wind, Trask continued to ride far too quickly down the over-grown route. The thought that if he slowed up a man or perhaps a family might lose their lives kept him charging on. Branches tore at him and his horse's flesh as they rode on. Trask ducked as tree limbs suddenly appeared before him in the dark avenue but he continued urging the creature onward into the sweet-smelling trail.

Then as he turned a tight corner with tree branches reaching out as if trying to touch the sky that lay above the green canopy, Trask felt the painful impact catching him squarely in the centre of his chest. The force was so great he found himself catapulted into the air, flying backward as his horse rode on without him. Trask had never been so scared in all his life as he felt himself ploughing head first through the undergrowth. It was dark where he was headed. His body seemed to be ripping its way through every conceiv-able sort of plant as he crashed down heavily onto the ground. It was as if every ounce of air was kicked from his lungs as he screwed his eyes up tightly.

The pain which overwhelmed him was unlike anything he had ever experienced in all his days.

Trask's neck seemed to take the full impact as he smashed into the wet ground. Desperately he opened his eyes trying to see where he was but nothing seemed real to his blurred brain. His eyes remained open long enough to see himself sliding backwards down a slippery slope. Then he felt the ice-cold water all about his body. He reached out vainly as he felt his head spinning wildly before everything went suddenly dark. Trask lay on his back in the shallow water unconscious. His faithful mount, Smoke, returned and stood looking down through the broken branches at its master and started to whinny uncontrollably.

★   ★   ★

Trask had no idea how long he had been unconscious in the river when his eyes eventually opened. The nose of his horse was right in his face snorting at him. He knew then it had been Smoke's doing he had woken up and reached for the bridle with both hands. His fingers were numb with the cold of the continuous flowing of the shallow river but he still had enough feeling to grab hold tightly onto the bridle. Smoke raised his strong neck and pulled its owner out of the water before stepping backwards until all four of its hooves were on the dry land of the embankment. Only then did the faithful stallion lower his head again and allow the man to rest on the wild grass. Trask released his grip and his arms fell limply to the ground.

He lay there for hours trying to regain his faculties.

17

'We done as you wanted, Davis,' Todd Fern said, as he emptied the remaining drops from his whiskey bottle and paced across the wide room in the large house belonging to the assayer. 'Now it's your turn to either pay us a further five hundred bucks or we up and hightail it out of here.'

Giles Davis stood against his desk studying the four ruthless men whom he had hired to assist him in his murderous plot. None of them had any idea of the wealth beneath their feet and he was not about to tell them. 'How do you figure I owe you another five hundred, Fern?'

'We done killed the folks on two farms. Right?'

Davis shrugged and opened the drawer of his desk and pulled out a money-box. 'I don't think I've got another five hundred dollars in cash here.'

Tubbs moved closer, eating the meal he had just taken from the kitchen. As he chewed he gave no thought to his murderous deeds only what lay on the plate in his hand. 'We gonna get paid or are we heading out, Fern?'

Davis took a small key from his vest pocket and unlocked the small box. 'I'll give you what I have in here but you boys will have to wait for me to get some more cash.'

Sonny Evans moved around the four men in the room as if wondering who or what he could kill next. 'Pay up, Davis. We kept our part of the bargain.'

'He's right,' the cool Jeff Leeming agreed. 'We either get our money or we are out of here.'

Davis stared into the eyes of Todd Fern as he pulled out the handful of bills. 'This is all I've got on the farm, Fern.'

Fern grabbed the money and

counted it quickly. 'Two hundred and twenty dollars.'

'That ain't enough,' Tubbs said, as food dropped from his mouth onto the polished floor.

Fern shook his head as he stuffed the money into his jeans pocket. 'Sorry, Davis.'

Davis moved towards the four men as they made their way to the door leading to the courtyard where all five of their mounts were tied. 'Come on, boys. I'll get the cash tomorrow. I gotta ride to Fairbanks to get the money.'

Todd Fern continued walking until the sun hit his face on the porch. 'Ain't good enough.'

Davis grabbed the taller man by the arm and swung him around to face him. 'I've hired you and you gotta stay.'

Evans, Leeming and Tubbs walked past Fern and Davis and moved down the steps to their horses. They mounted and watched their leader eye to eye with the sly Davis. It was clear that neither of the pair considered they were going to lose this disagreement but Fern had the advantage. He could shoot his way out of most problems.

'You let go of my arm or you'll end up deader than the folks we torched earlier.' Todd Fern glared at Giles Davis with eyes that conveyed the simple truth. He was not joking.

Davis felt his grip loosen as the words burned into him. 'Look, Fern, I can get money tomorrow. Stick around or ride with me to Fairbanks now.'

The ruthless Fern stared down at his boots as he considered the request. 'Me and the boys can't go back to Fairbanks because we kinda had a bit of trouble there, Davis.'

'Then wait here whilst I go and get the money.' There was a terror in the man's voice that did not sit well with the four gunmen.

Fern ran down the steps; and grabbed his reins as he mounted the horse. 'I tell you what, Mr Davis,' he began, 'we'll go to Coffeeville and drink the town dry. You can go to Fairbanks and get the money. We'll come back here tonight when we are good and liquored up. We'll wait for you to get back here.'

The assayer knew that was as good as it was going to get with these hard-nosed killers. All they wanted was money. Anyone's money. There was no loyalty amongst their sort. Davis stood open-mouthed as he watched the four men turn their horses and dig their spurs deeply into the flesh of the poor creatures beneath their saddles. The men headed out onto the trail leading to the small township. Sweat dripped from his face as he wondered how he could get enough cash together to keep these men quiet. Entering the house again he moved quickly into his library where the walls were filled with expensive volumes of books, most of which he had never even read. On the far wall he slid a panel across the third shelf revealing a small combination safe. Carefully turning the wheel four times until he heard a faint clicking noise, Davis then turned the small handle down sharply and pulled the door open. Wiping the sweat off his face he withdrew a bag and paced to the window where a small table stood catching the light upon its polished surface.

Davis loosened the drawstring and poured the contents onto the table. Eighteen gold nuggets gleamed up at his face. That had to be enough, he thought.

It had to be enough. He had not had enough time to gather more nuggets since his guests had arrived. One by one he placed the golden stones back into the small bag. In Fairbanks he would be able to turn these into hard cash.

* * *

Spitting a mixture of blood and vomit from his mouth Trask grovelled on his knees trying to remember what had happened to him. It had been like a terrible nightmare yet every sinew in his body ached so intently he knew it had been no mere dream. Trask looked up at the sun as its light splintered through the canopy of branches and leaves. He knew that it was far higher now than when he was last conscious meaning many hours must have passed by without him noticing. He crawled to the edge of the fast-flowing, crystal-clear river and scooped out a handful of the liquid to wash off his face. The shock of the icy water on his face and neck cleared not only his eyes but his mind. Trask dropped his face into the river and drank feverishly. He lay on his knees watching the water until his vision returned to its original sharpness.

Gazing down past his own reflection he saw something only inches beneath the surface of the water. Trask felt his stomach churning as realization struck him: shining stones that glinted brightly in the filtered rays of the sun which managed to penetrate the millions of leaves above him. Trask reached into the cold water and picked up the largest stone and studied it carefully. Its golden brilliance carved its way into his brain as he pulled himself back up onto his knees.

'Gold,' Trask mumbled, showing the nugget to his horse. 'That's what all this has been about, Smoke. Gold.'

Scrambling to his feet he stood holding onto his saddle trying to figure out whether he was truly in one piece. The golden stone in his hand seemed to taunt him as he stared at it with eyes that cursed its existence, cursed the value other men placed upon the ore that had no real use. This was why the people were being slain in this nameless valley. Trask tossed the nugget away and tried to establish if he had any broken bones which might hamper his continuing. Everything seemed OK if badly bruised. He knew that Giles Davis was an assayer and must have realized the entire valley was literally a gold mine waiting for someone like him to exploit. Others might have chosen a different way to harvest the hidden wealth that lay waiting to be reaped, but Davis had decided to kill his way to riches. Running his thumb-nail over the gun-belt on the saddle horn he stared at the branded words that spelled out the name of Trask. For the first time in the two decades since he had first purchased the very special shooting rig, he actually felt as if he were Trask.

Stooping, Trask plucked his ripped Stetson off the ground at his feet and placed it carefully onto his sore head. Gathering up the loose reins he led Smoke up the steep incline back onto the narrow trail before stepping into the stirrup and pulling himself into the saddle. He sat motionless for what seemed an eternity trying to calm himself for the job ahead. However hard he tried, he knew the shining golden stones had worked their evil and claimed the lives of people he liked. To a man like Trask it just didn't seem to make any sense at all.

Trask looked at the two eagle-butt

grips of his guns and then up at the trail
ahead of his tall horse. He knew what
he had to do and rode ahead at a
normal pace ready to do it. Now only
he could serve justice and bring an end
to this. He was alone again, but he had
grown used to that. Now he was the law
and these people's only hope of
salvation.

The chestnut stallion trotted along
the trail with Trask sitting in the saddle
silently holding his reins in one hand as
the other stroked the grips of his guns.
He had been lying in the river for a very
long time by the sun above the tree
canopy. It had to be the middle of the
afternoon by the height of the brilliant
orb. He gritted his teeth as the thought
of the people at the Johnson farm filled
his mind. He would have to ride there
and see the damage Davis and his gang
had done. Now there was no reason for
haste. Whatever evil deed Davis and his
men had been up to, Trask knew he had
been knocked out for too long to be of
any help to them. As his horse

continued down the narrow avenue he felt death must have already struck again.

★ ★ ★

The Johnson farmhouse was no more. The smell of burning had filled his nostrils long before he had reached the smouldering shell. Trask drew up his reins and gazed in horror at the sight before him. He looked around for any signs of life but there was none to be either seen or salvaged. Helplessly he rode around the blackened smoking timbers and the stone chimney looking for anyone he might help, but it was clear, after only a few minutes, he was far too late. This had happened hours before his arrival and if any bodies existed he knew they must be under the ashes of what once had been a home.

It took him many minutes of just circling the destroyed farmhouse before he was able to convince himself of the fact he could do nothing here.

Trask rubbed his eyes and sucked in air through his teeth before digging his spurs into the horse and riding away from the tragic scene. Within minutes he was on the trail and heading down the wider route he had used when entering this valley for the first time. As he rode he could see the chewed-up ground of many riders. This had been the way Davis and his gang had come and gone, he thought. The route he should have chosen.

Riding harder and harder Trask began to feel true hatred burning into his guts. The chestnut reacted to every signal its master gave. Galloping down the dusty road the gunfighter began to be overcome by a mixture of fury and vengeance. All he could think of was the face of Giles Davis. All he could think about was killing the man who had caused such mayhem. Trask had never before been overwhelmed by such torrid emotions and yet it drove him on. The chestnut stallion ate up the trail faster than any horse had done before.

Within an hour, Trask had covered the distance between the Johnson farm and the gates of the Davis spread. Trask pulled his horse to a violent halt before quickly dismounting. Every sense that had protected him for more than forty years seemed to be fully alert as he surveyed the scene. Twenty yards ahead was the turning that led up to the huge house belonging to the assayer, whilst to his side the closely spaced trees and dark shadows offered cover from observers. Trask took the reins, walking the lathered-up chestnut into the shadows.

The sky had darkened during his ride and Trask studied the heavens as he washed his mouth clean with his canteen. The sun was now low and fighting with the encroaching clouds for domination. He figured that there was only another two hours at best of daylight remaining. Two hours would normally be enough time to do what he had to do yet these were not normal circumstances. Trask had never felt the pain of loss before.

Trask stood looking at the gun-belt before taking it off the saddle horn and unbuckling it. Staring at the house through the trees he pulled it around his middle and slid the leather strap through the silver buckle. He pulled it to its tightest notch before stooping and tying the leather laces that hung from each holster around his broad thighs. Straightening up he took off his hat and hung it over the saddle horn with a deep sigh. For an instant he felt weak and stumbled before regaining his balance long enough to catch his breath.

The injuries he had sustained earlier might have been worse than he had first imagined. Rubbing his face he noticed blood on his hand. His nose was bleeding. He checked it but it appeared to be unbroken. The blood could be a warning of something far worse yet the gunfighter shrugged off any concerns for his own health. He had a job to do and nothing could deter him from completing his task.

Trask turned and faced the house again trying to focus his mind on the chore ahead. He sniffed and then spat out more blood before starting to make his way through the trees.

With every stride he felt stronger. Flicking the safety loops off the gun hammers he started to toy with the unique weapons as if trying to awaken them for the action ahead.

The undergrowth gave him ample cover as he made his way through the trees towards the rear of the building. He finally reached the edge of the tree-line and halted his progress whilst he looked at the gap between where he stood and the house. It was only thirty or more feet. Twenty years earlier he would have dashed across such a gap in a split second. Now he knew it would take longer.

Trask bent over and ran at the rear door of the great house and did not stop until he found the back wall. As he leaned against the wall he noticed small droplets of blood falling at his feet. Standing upright he tilted his head back and rubbed his face along the back of his sleeve. Something was wrong, he concluded, but what?

A sudden noise from inside the utility room made him draw both his guns. Now sweat as well as blood fell from his face as his fingers clutched the two pistols. Footsteps were coming closer and closer across the floor of the room. Trask pulled the hammers back with his thumbs until they locked.

18

The female servant stood staring down the barrels of the two beautiful guns in Trask's hands. Her face showed little sign of either fear or concern.

'You again?' she said in recognition of the man she had encountered earlier, the man who had spoken to her as if she were more than a mere washer woman.

Trask shook his head and lowered the pistols. His face was apologetic as he leaned into the wall. 'I'm sorry, honey.' He sighed heavily.

She placed her hard-skinned hands around his face and stared into his eyes. 'You are hurt, mister.'

'I figured that, ma'am.' Trask tried to smile but the bitter taste of vengeance soured his natural instincts. 'Where is Davis and the bastards working for him?'

Her face seemed troubled by his condition as she helped him into the cool room. She raised her index finger to his lips.

Trask holstered one gun and took her arm. 'Where are they?' he whispered.

Moving her face close to his ear she spoke in hushed tones. 'My master is in the big room full of books. The other men had words with him and rode off to town.'

Trask felt a sudden rush of energy filling his aching body as he nodded at her. Touching the woman's cheek he moved silently past her through the kitchen until he came to the vaulted ceiling of the hall. His energy seemed to come and go at an alarming speed. One moment he was feeling strong and the next weak. As he moved he listened. Then his ears detected the sound of movement to his left. Turning he paused for a second before striding towards the library.

Giles Davis was hastily filling a saddle-bag as the gunfighter entered, holding his right-hand pistol at waist height. The man stared up to see the familiar figure facing him. Davis froze as his jaw dropped in shock.

'Trask,' he gasped almost disbelieving his eyes. 'I thought you had left the valley.'

Trask moved slowly towards the man waving his gun at the assayer. 'You must be the lowest critter this side of Hell, Davis.'

The neat man walked away from the saddle-bags where he had put the bag of gold nuggets and a few clothes for the trip to Fairbanks. 'What's eating you, Trask?'

Trask spun his gun into its holster before clenching his fists in anger. 'You going on a trip?'

Davis tried to keep the distance between them moving sideways across the room as Trask closed in on him. 'I heard about the fire at the Hart farmhouse. Tragic.'

Trask stopped and stared down at the highly polished floor. It was shining so it seemed to be almost like a mirror. 'You killed two fine people, Davis. You and your henchmen.'

Davis moved behind a large couch. 'I had nothing to do with the death of Cooper or the Hart girl.'

Trask looked up through his eyebrows at the man before him and gritted his teeth. 'Gold nuggets. You killed all these folks in the valley because of gold nuggets, Davis. I figure that you thought you could get rid of the people and then harvest yourself a mighty profitable crop.'

The face of the elegant Davis suddenly went pale as he realized Trask had figured it all out. 'What are you gonna do to me, Trask?'

Trask shook his head and felt the trickle of blood dripping from his nose. He watched as it hit the floor at his feet then looked up in the deplorable man's direction. 'I figure that you are better dead than alive, Davis.'

'You would shoot me in cold-blood?' Davis stared across the room at his own gun-belt hanging over a high-back chair next to the famous gunfighter. 'I ain't even armed.'

Trask picked up Davis's gun-belt and tossed it across the wide library. It landed upon the couch where Davis stood. 'Put it on you deadbeat.'

Giles Davis felt the sweat running down his face as he tried to think of a way out of this situation. Death was facing him and he knew it would claim him if he could not think of an answer to his perilous situation. 'You ain't known as a cold-blooded murderer, Trask. Are you a murderer?'

'God knows what I am,' Trask said walking towards the saddle-bags as if drawn by a magnet. 'I'll answer to Him and nobody else, Davis.'

Davis watched as the man flicked the strap of the bulging bag. 'You want to make yourself rich, Trask?'

Trask looked across at the sweat-soaked Davis. 'Nope,' he sighed.

'Look inside the bag,' Davis stammered. 'Just take a look inside the bag.'

Trask pulled out the garments from the saddle-bags and dropped them onto the floor before finding the small bag full of nuggets and withdrawing them. 'Heavy.'

'That bag has eighteen large gold nuggets inside it, Trask,' Davis said fearfully. 'It's yours if you spare my life.'

Trask tossed the bag up into the air as if checking the weight of its contents before catching it. 'Eighteen nuggets?'

'Worth hundreds perhaps thousands of dollars.'

Trask placed the small bag onto the table and squared up to the man. 'I was gonna kill you like the mad dog you are when I arrived, Davis.' He spat his words at the man. 'Now I'm just ashamed that I almost came down to your level. I almost swam in the same sewer as you and your hired rats.'

For the first time since he had set eyes upon the gunfighter, Davis felt as if he might just live to see the sun setting once more. 'You ain't gonna kill me, Trask?'

Trask turned and headed slowly towards the door that led to the hallway. 'I wouldn't waste lead on scum like you. I'll let the folks in Coffeeville lynch you, if that's their choice.'

Davis watched as the man slowly ambled towards the stained door of his library. Then he saw the man sway as if injured. His eyes stared down at the gun-belt on the soft padded couch before him. Trask was showing nothing but his broad back to the assayer as if in a trance.

Unable to resist the open target, Davis reached over the back of the couch and pulled his Colt from its holster and raised it, taking aim at the man's spine. Pulling the trigger, Davis lost sight of Trask in the cloud of gunsmoke that blasted from his gun barrel. What he had not seen as his finger squeezed the trigger was Trask stumbling to the floor a split second before the bullet left the barrel.

Trask was on his knees as the bullet passed over his head and embedded itself into the bookcase before him. Turning and drawing his guns he returned fire twice without even knowing how he managed to do so. His head cleared and he stared at the two outheld weapons in his hands. It was as if they had fired themselves to the gunfighter who had no memory of pulling the triggers himself.

As the room cleared of the gunsmoke, Trask remained on his knees as blood ran freely from his nostrils again. He was dazed and confused but the sight of Giles Davis lying lifelessly over the upholstered couch made him realize his enemy was dead.

The woman from the rear of the building rushed into the room and surveyed the scene with eyes that seemed to have witnessed many things in her half-century of life. She helped Trask back to his feet and used her apron to wipe the blood from his face.

'Thank you, ma'am,' Trask said weakly.

'You killed him,' she said in a voice which seemed almost grateful.

'You lost your job I guess. I'm sorry.' Trask took deep breaths as she poured him a brandy and made him take some. It seemed to help as he found his eyes clearing.

'He was a really bad man.' She spat across the room at the body. 'He did many bad things.'

'You said the other men headed into town?' Trask searched her face for answers.

'Yes, mister. They headed to Coffeeville,' she replied.

Trask touched her cheek softly. He knew that hard work had lined her face and she had probably never had more than a few cents at any one time in her entire life. Then he had an idea that cheered him as he straightened up. Trask strode to the table and lifted the small bag full of gold nuggets and gave them to the woman. 'Take these and get away from here.'

'What is this?'

'Gold nuggets,' Trask said, as he walked across the hallway and out into the sunlight. He turned and smiled at her. 'I reckon you could say it's your retirement pay, honey.'

19

The four men had been drinking in the small saloon for two hours and getting more and more bored. This was not the sort of drinking hole they were accustomed to. This place was clean and quiet and lacked anything a real saloon offered apart from hard liquor. Boredom in the hands of the average man was bad enough, but in the hands of scum like Fern and company, it was dangerous.

The old bartender had watched what he was saying to the four men who had more weaponry covering their clothing than he had ever seen before. They had already consumed four bottles of his best Scotch between them since they had arrived just before sunset. The few regular customers had all gone when they had seen these men stride in with their hands filled with cash.

The clock above the bar started to strike the quarter-hour and all four men looked up at it. It chimed loud and clear as if warning of something yet to happen.

Sonny Evans was edgy and nervous and wanted a woman, any woman. He had a problem that the others did not share. He liked to sew his oats as often as possible. This was not the saloon for such a man.

'Quit shaking, Sonny,' Leeming said, as the younger man kept tapping his hands on the bar top, his foot rattling on the brass foot rest.

'There any whorehouses in this town, old man?' Evans croaked over his drink.

The old bartender raised both eyebrows in total shock at the question. 'Not a single one,' he replied.

'Why not?' Evans was trying to get to grips with the fact that he wanted something that simply was not available. 'You must have a place for menfolk to go.'

'Sorry.' The bartender shook his head

as he polished glasses and watched the men before him.

Fern glanced across at his men. 'Take it easy, boys.'

Tubbs continued to eat the food the old man had placed on the counter. 'I don't wanna woman.'

'Me neither,' Leeming shrugged.

'Quit looking at me,' Sonny Evans growled. 'I wanna woman and if you boys don't then that just ain't natural.'

Fern raised a finger at the man who was getting far more anxious than he ought. 'Quit getting yourself all worked up and enjoy your drink.'

Evans pulled himself away from the bar and rubbed both hands over his face. 'You drink. I'm going for a walk. There has to be a female somewhere in this damn town.'

Todd Fern faced the younger gang member. 'Where you thinking of walking, Sonny?'

Evans spat into the spittoon at his feet and smiled. 'If there's a woman out there I'll find her, Fern.'

His three companions watched as he marched out of the saloon into the darkness.

'Take it easy, Fern,' said Tubbs, still chewing. 'He's hot and when he's hot he's damn dangerous.'

Fern picked up his glass and swallowed the Scotch. 'If there ain't no whorehouses here what's he gonna do for a woman?'

The two men shrugged and faced the mirror.

There were no answers that could be given.

20

The coal-oil lamps tried vainly to illuminate the street as the three men staggered out onto the sidewalk. They had drunk their fill of the town's best liquor and decided to head back to the sanctuary of Giles Davis's farm. Fern stood stretching as Leeming and Tubbs attempted to untie their reins from the hitching rail before him.

The night air was cool as it drifted down the long street and chilled the three men's bones. Then they saw the rider sitting motionless on his chestnut stallion outside the livery stable. The moonlight cast a blue haze over the man who was just watching them.

'Who is that, Fern?' Tubbs asked quietly as he stared over the saddle of his horse.

Leeming pulled himself up to his full height and looked at where the fat gunman was pointing. 'Yeah, who is that?'

Todd Fern looked down the street and felt sweat running down his back. 'Damn,' he muttered when he stepped down beside his two companions.

'Who is it, Fern?' Tubbs asked again, as the tall man moved next to him.

'Trask!' Fern mumbled in a voice that verged on panic.

They watched as Trask allowed his mount to start to walk towards them. When the horse had reached the white picket fence of Doc Vale's, he reined in and dismounted.

Slapping the tail of the tall chestnut, Trask stood silently as his horse trotted past them.

Each of the three looked at one another.

'What should we do, Fern?' Jeff Leeming gulped, as he gazed in awe at the man standing in the centre of the dark street.

'We ought to run,' Tubbs said, shaking.

Fern took a lungful of air and stepped away from their horses and looked at the man hard. It was certainly Trask, he mused. An older, greyer Trask than he remembered. 'We can take him, boys.'

Tubbs and Leeming walked beside their leader reluctantly watching the old man standing alone before them.

'He's an old man,' Fern said under his breath. 'Look at him. He's old.'

Tubbs rubbed his drink-weary eyes. 'You're right, Fern. He is old.'

'Does that mean we can take him?' Leeming rubbed his chin as he weighed up the situation.

Before any of the trio could say another word, Trask stepped two paces forward and pushed his Stetson up off his face. 'You the scum Giles Davis hired?'

Fern advanced one stride. 'We are.'

'Then I gotta inform you he's dead.' Trask spat blood from his mouth onto the road.

Fern felt a sudden chill moving over

him. Suddenly Trask's appearance seemed to be less important. 'You kill him, Trask?'

Trask took another step. 'I did.'

'Let's get out of here, Fern,' Leeming suggested loudly.

Trask watched as all three men moved apart trying to make themselves harder targets to hit. As he watched them he wondered where the fourth man was.

'We ain't got no problem with you, Trask!' Fern shouted. 'You head out and we'll not draw on you.'

'Sorry,' Trask said coldly, watching the men as black clouds rolled overhead, obliterating the moon every few seconds. 'I have got to stop you boys from killing anyone else.'

'Why?' Tubbs shouted angrily. 'You ain't the law, old man.'

Trask flexed his fingers. 'There ain't no law, fatman. So I just elected myself judge, jury and executioner.'

The three men froze to the ground as they watched Trask begin to slowly walk towards them. This was no ordinary gunfighter facing them. This was the legendary Trask. The man with the mysterious guns, guns which were said to be able to fire themselves.

Fern drew first quickly followed by his two men. Trask's hands seemed to move to his gun grips without him even losing a step as he drew. Bullets lit up the dark street as they cut through the air like lightning bolts.

Within seconds of the battle beginning it had ended in a bloodbath. Only Trask remained standing as the lights within the houses around him began to be lighted by the citizens of Coffeeville awoken from their slumbers.

Trask stared at the three bodies before him as he had done so many times in the past and then at the smoking barrels of his famed pistols. Once again they had done what had to be done with deadly accuracy. Slowly he holstered them as he heard the familiar voice of Doc Vale behind him.

'Trask! Trask!' the doctor shouted, desperately trying to get his attention.

As the gunfighter turned around to face the man, he saw the figure of Sonny Evans standing at the end of the street clutching his two cocked .45s.

Trask stood watching as the last of the killers snarled as he approached. The words were lost in the chilling wind which whipped down the centre of the dark avenue. Trask might not have been able to understand what the kid was yelling but he knew exactly what he meant.

Trask held up his right hand as if vainly trying to stop the young killer. 'Holster them Colts, boy,' he urged.

'So you are the famous Trask,' Evans shouted as people began to open their front doors and venture out on either side of the street.

'Quit now son,' Trask shouted lowering his arm.

Sonny Evans was in no mood to quit. He was hot and had been unable to find himself comfort with a female either living or dead as he had done with the young Juliette Hart days earlier. This was not a man but a crazed animal who waved his guns at the older injured Trask. 'You killed my friends but I got your woman,' Evans bragged. 'I got her good. I gave her what she wanted and even when she was dead and gone I gave her more, Trask.'

Trask's face went blank as the words carved themselves into his heart. 'You killed Juliette?'

'I did more than just kill her,' Evans laughed as he started firing his guns at the gunfighter's feet. 'I gave her what you were too old to give her.'

As the ground at Trask's feet was being blasted by the bullets from Evans's guns, Trask felt the two eagle-butt Peacemakers in his hands. He felt his fingers hardly touching the triggers as the bullets blasted from the barrels out into the darkness. He felt his fingers still squeezing the triggers long after the chambers were empty.

The sight of Sonny Evans riddled with his bullets made no difference to him as he holstered the guns and started to walk away. Then he felt himself hitting the ground and staring through blurred eyes as Doc Vale and the other citizens of Coffeeville rushed towards him. Trask then felt himself falling into a place where nightmares ruled and dreams died.

Finale

The good people of Coffeeville treated the injured Trask like the saviour he was during the weeks he spent in bed at Doc Vale's place recovering from his injuries.

When he was finally allowed back onto his feet he had been given every honour these people could think of. To them he was a hero and they wanted him to stay with them in their beautiful valley. Trask had no memory of most of what had occurred during his heroic fight with Davis and his men. Even the venomous words spat from the mouth of Sonny Evans had been forgotten by a mind unable to cope with their ugliness. The doctor diagnosed Trask had fractured his skull when he had been knocked from his saddle on the way to the Johnson place. Only rest had stopped the nosebleeds and allowed his body to heal itself.

The town now knew why so many of the valley's people had been killed by Davis and his henchmen. Yet they seemed unconcerned by the fact that their valley was littered with gold. Like Trask himself, they held no value for the precious ore and feared what might happen if the news ever reached the outside world.

Then came the day when Trask knew that he was fully mended, and almost back to his old self. Standing by the white picket fence he said nothing as the townspeople greeted him. He smiled the smile of a man who knew that this was truly a paradise once more and yet did not gloat in the fact he was responsible for its return.

'You going to stay, Trask?' Doc Vale asked, placing a hand on the wide shoulder.

Trask glanced at the man. 'What would I do here, Doc?'

'We need a sheriff,' the man replied.

'No you don't,' Trask sighed. 'Now

there's peace in the valley again.'

'Thanks to you, man.'

'Maybe.'

'For how long will peace remain here if the news of the gold gets out, Trask?' Vale's face studied the gunfighter.

'Maybe forever.'

There was a long silence as the tall gunfighter tried to find a reason for his feeling so sad. Then he entered the small house and returned holding the gun-belt with the name 'Trask' branded onto it. He put the buckled belt over his shoulder and stood beside the doctor for a moment.

'You are leaving?' Vale gasped. 'Why, man? Why?'

Trask shrugged as he watched the muscular figure of Matt Hume leading his saddled chestnut stallion towards them. 'I asked Matt earlier if he would bring Smoke to me, Doc.'

'Why, Trask?' Vale could not understand. 'We want you to stay here with us. You above all men have earned the right.'

Trask opened the white gate and looped the gun-belt over the saddle horn before taking the reins from the butcher. 'I'm not the right sort to live with decent folks, Doc.'

As Trask mounted the tall horse people from every building gathered around him. Each and every one of them had eyes that longed for him to remain in Coffeeville, to stay in their sweet valley and live alongside them.

'You could have the Hart Farm, Trask.' Jack Smith the barber said as everyone nodded in agreement. 'Or any of the other farms left empty by Davis and his men. Stay.'

'Stay, Trask,' Vale pleaded with the man he had brought back from the brink of death only weeks earlier.

Trask looked at the faces below him. Good faces belonging to souls unmatched anywhere in the West. 'I thank you all for being so kind to me, but there's one thing you are forgetting.'

'What?' Matt Hume asked, staring up

at the man in the saddle.

Trask tapped the guns before him. 'These.'

'What about them?' Vale cleared his throat. 'They are just guns, son. Just guns.'

Trask nodded. 'They are the guns of Trask. They will attract men far worse than any Davis hired. They'll destroy your valley, maybe not today or tomorrow but some day. I couldn't allow that to happen to you folks.'

Without allowing any of their arguments to reach his ears for fear that they might persuade him to defy his own judgement and remain in this beautiful place, Trask pulled his horse away from them. He thought about the face of the lovely Hart girl and wondered if he might have made a different decision had she not been slain. For a brief moment in his long life he had seen the face of a woman he could have loved. Juliette Hart had died and so had his soul. Without her to keep him here, he knew he must continue his search for peace elsewhere.

The gentle tapping of Trask's feet gave Smoke the signal to start walking. The people of Coffeeville watched silently as the man who had saved their community from the greed of ruthless killers rode slowly down the street and headed away along the lush tree-lined trail. Whatever the truth of the matter concerning his guns, they would never set eyes upon the man known simply as Trask again. He was aiming Smoke towards newer, fresher pastures with the same two silver dollars in his jacket pocket he had arrived with.

A TOWN CALLED
TROUBLESOME

John Dyson

Matt Matthews had carved his ranch out of the wild Wyoming frontier. But he had his troubles. The big blow of '86 was catastrophic, with dead beeves littering the plains, and the oncoming winter presaged worse. On top of this, a gang of desperadoes had moved into the Snake River valley, killing, raping and rustling. All Matt can do is to take on the killers singlehanded. But will he escape the hail of lead?

BRAZOS STATION

Clayton Nash

Caleb Brett liked his job as deputy sheriff and being betrothed to the sheriff's daughter, Rose. What he didn't like was the thought of the sheriff moving in with them once they were married. But capturing the infamous outlaw Gil Bannerman offered a way out because there was plenty of reward money. Then came Brett's big mistake — he lost Bannerman and was framed. Now everything he treasured was lost. Did he have a chance in hell of fighting his way back?

DEAD IS FOR EVER

Amy Sadler

After rescuing Hope Bennett from the clutches of two trailbums, Sam Carver made a serious mistake. He killed one of the outlaws, and reckoned on collecting the bounty on Lew Daggett. But catching Sam off-guard, Daggett made off with the girl, leaving Sam for dead. However, he was only grazed and once he came to, he set out in search of Hope. When he eventually found her, he was forced into a dramatic showdown with his life on the line.

SMOKING STAR

B. J. Holmes

In the one-horse town of Medicine Bluff two men were dead. Sheriff Jack Starr didn't need the badge on his chest to spur him into tracking the killer. He had his own reason for seeking justice, a reason no-one knew. It drove him to take a journey into the past where he was to discover something else that was to add even greater urgency to the situation — to stop Montana's rivers running red with blood.

THE WIND WAGON

Troy Howard

Sheriff Al Corning was as tough as they came and with his four seasoned deputies he kept the peace in Laramie — at least until the squatters came. To fend off starvation, the settlers took some cattle off the cowmen, including Jonas Lefler. A hard, unforgiving man, Lefler retaliated with lynchings. Things got worse when one of the squatters revealed he was a former Texas lawman — and no mean shooter. Could Sheriff Corning prevent further bloodshed?